What Reviewers Say About Bold Strokes Books' Authors

❧

KIM BALDWIN

"Her…crisply written action scenes, juxtaposition of smart dialogue make this a story the reader will absolutely enjoy and long remember." – **Arlene Germain**, book reviewer for the *Lambda Book Report* and the *Midwest Book Review*

❧

ROSE BEECHAM

"…a mystery writer with a delightful sense of humor, as well as an eye for an interesting array of characters…" – *MegaScene*

"…her characters seem fully capable of walking away from the particulars of whodunit and engaging the reader in other aspects of their lives." – *Lambda Book Report*

"…creates believable characters in compelling situations, with enough humor to provide effective counterpoint to the work of detecting." – *Bay Area Reporter*

❧

JANE FLETCHER

"…a natural gift for rich storytelling and world-building…one of the best fantasy writers at work today." – **Jean Stewart**, author of the *Isis* series

❧

RADCLY*f*FE

"Powerful characters, engrossing plot, and intelligent writing…" – **Cameron Abbott,** author of *To the Edge* and *An Inexpressible State of Grace*

"…well-honed storytelling skills…solid prose and sure-handedness of the narrative…" – **Elizabeth Flynn**, *Lambda Book Report*

"…well-plotted…lovely romance…I couldn't turn the pages fast enough!" – **Ann Bannon**, author of *The Beebo Brinker Chronicles.*

"…a consummate artist in crafting classic romance fiction…her numerous best selling works exemplify the splendor and power of Sapphic passion…" – **Yvette Murray, PhD**, *Reader's Raves*

Love's Melody Lost

by

RADCLYfFE

2005

ISBN 1-933110-00-7

THIS TRADE PAPERBACK ORIGINAL IS PUBLISHED BY
BOLD STROKES BOOKS, INC.,
PHILADELPHIA, PA, USA

FIRST PRINTING, 2001
SECOND PRINTING, 2002
THIRD PRINTING, 2003
FOURTH PRINTING: AUGUST, 2004, BOLD STROKES BOOKS, INC.
FIFTH PRINTING: JUNE, 2005, BOLD STROKES BOOKS, INC.

CREDITS
PRODUCTION DESIGN: J. BARRE GREYSTONE
COVER DESIGN BY SHERI (GRAPHICARTIST2020@HOTMAIL.COM)

By the Author

Romances

Safe Harbor

Beyond the Breakwater

Innocent Hearts

Love's Melody Lost

Love's Tender Warriors

Tomorrow's Promise

Passion's Bright Fury

Love's Masquerade

shadowland

Fated Love

Distant Shores, Silent Thunder

Honor Series

Above All, Honor

Honor Bound

Love & Honor

Honor Guards

Justice Series

A Matter of Trust (prequel)

Shield of Justice

In Pursuit of Justice

Justice in the Shadows

Justice Served

Change Of Pace: *Erotic Interludes*
(A Short Story Collection)

Author's Note

I am often asked to name my favorite characters from my own writings, and of course that is impossible because each holds a unique place in my heart. When cornered however, Graham is one of the two I name. In the chronology of my works as written (as opposed to published), this book is number three, between *shadowland* and *Safe Harbor.*

Radclyffe 2005

Dedication

For Lee, For Daring to Dream

CHAPTER ONE

Anna Reid drove with one hand holding a torn scrap of paper against the wheel. As she watched for road signs in the unfamiliar back roads of Cape Cod Bay, she tried to decipher her own scribbled writing. The early spring morning was unseasonably warm, and she had put the old Jeep's canvas top down to enjoy the sun. The breeze that blew through her hair smelled of salt water, seaweed and ocean creatures. It was a welcome change from the heavy air and city smells she had grown used to in Boston over the years. So much in her life had changed—too much for her to think about without stirring all her misgivings about this present strange venture. She reminded herself silently that she had made many hard decisions in the last months and she could not turn back now, not with her last hope so near.

Anna eventually turned onto a narrow, twisting, tree-lined lane that led to a large old Victorian edifice. Four stories, replete with gables and porticos, it stood alone on a bluff above the sea. The circular drive in front was cracked in places with clumps of vegetation attempting to displace the offending concrete. The house also showed signs of disrepair. Shutters hung askew, paint curled from the wood surfaces, and several windows on the upper stories were boarded over. She frowned at the overgrown formal gardens that clearly had not been tended in years. There was an air of sadness reflected in the decline of this once beautiful estate, and Anna felt herself immediately drawn to the place. It was as if it were a living presence, long-neglected and in need of care. She pulled to a stop before the grand staircase, ascending to a wide verandah. She approached the pair of heavy ornate oak doors with a mixture of excitement and trepidation. She took a deep breath as she rang the bell.

Slowly, the doors creaked open and a small gray-haired woman peered up at her.

"Yes?" the woman inquired uncertainly.

"I'm Anna Reid. I was hired by Mr. Norcross as a housekeeper."

The little woman's face broke into a thousand tiny lines as she smiled and extended her hand. "I am Helen Green, and *I*, my dear, am the housekeeper. *You* are here to manage our household business, and I am so glad you have arrived. Welcome to Yardley Manor."

Anna grasped her hand automatically, her mind in turmoil. "But, Mr. Norcross indicated—"

Helen pulled her inside, saying, "I'm sure that Mr. Norcross explained things as he knew them, but Graham is not very good at keeping the poor man informed. What we need, my dear, is someone to oversee the property as well as to manage Graham's personal affairs. Graham will explain it all to you later. Come with me now. Let me show you to your rooms."

Anna hung back in confusion. She recalled the ad she had answered from a Boston newspaper.

"Live-in house manager needed. Must do some clerical work and drive. Salary and schedule negotiable."

She had thought it odd that a senior attorney in one of Boston's most prestigious law firms had conducted the interview. When he informed her that the location was forty minutes outside of Boston and required little in the way of advanced secretarial skills, she had been encouraged. Her employer, she had learned after insistent probing, would be Graham Yardley, a former musician who lived in a secluded estate on the coast. David Norcross, the attorney who interviewed her, had been reluctant to provide much in the way of details, and Anna's curiosity had been piqued. When he went on to assure her that she would have ample opportunity to arrange her duties around her class schedule, she had accepted immediately, terminated her lease, and packed the essentials of her life.

She stared at the older woman who looked at her in pleased anticipation while her own anxiety escalated. What exactly was it she was supposed to do here? She had no experience in managing an estate, and from the brief glance she had had of Yardley Manor, it was definitely in need of managing. Still, she instinctively liked the spry elderly woman who hurried down the long hall to a wide central staircase, and what she could see of the house captured her attention immediately. Even in its current state of neglect, it was magnificent. As she followed the housekeeper through the dark mahogany-paneled hall, she caught glimpses of the adjoining rooms through partially opened doors. Thick imported carpets, brocade-covered sofas and opulent draperies graced the high-ceilinged rooms. Multi-faceted crystal chandeliers cast flickering shadows over highly polished, ornately carved tables and broad mantelpieces. Yardley Manor managed to project an air of elegance even in its present state.

"Perhaps I should speak with Mr. Yardley first," Anna suggested as Helen stopped before a door on the second floor. "There might be a problem. I'm not sure I'm going to be suitable for the job."

Helen turned toward her with a strangely quiet, penetrating gaze. "Graham will meet with you at tea this afternoon. The two of you can straighten all of this out then. Now, come my dear, and let me get you settled."

Anna realized that she had no choice but to wait. The room Helen led her into was bright and airy, and the floor to ceiling windows on the far side of the bed captured her attention immediately. They faced the heart of the estate—two hundred yards of terraced gardens which gave way to a tangle of wild brush growing up to the edge of a rocky bluff. A tiered stone wall rimmed the edge of the cliff, which fell a hundred feet down into the pounding surf. Beyond that was only the blue of sky and water. The view was breathtaking.

Anna could just make out the garden paths, now narrowed and overrun by the steady encroachment of natural flora untended for years. Here and there stone benches were still visible under the trees, marking the spots which had once provided strollers a place to rest and enjoy the surrounding beauty. To the rear left was a wide flagstone terrace, ringed by a stone balustrade which supported dozens of climbing rose bushes, desperately in need of pruning and cultivation. Beyond that stretched the formal rose gardens, clearly what had been the showpiece of the estate at one time. Now all she surveyed lay in ruins, a sad reminder of what had been, like a faded photograph of a time long gone. She was amazed to find her throat tighten around sudden tears, she was so moved by the decline of this once proud manor. It was such a waste, when all it needed was care. She shrugged her melancholy aside; she had her own life to worry about resurrecting. She turned back to the room she was hopefully going to inhabit.

"Oh," Anna exclaimed, observing the room closely for the first time. She was delighted to see a high canopied poster bed, lovely antique walnut dressers, and mirrored vanity table. Sconces on the walls still held candles, although the overhead stained-glass light and matching table lamps now provided the light. Underfoot, thick richly colored carpets covered the glossy wood floors. The interior of the house, clearly Helen's domain, had been lovingly maintained.

The neglected state of the exterior and grounds was clearly not from lack of funds. From what she had seen so far, most of the furnishings appeared to be priceless estate pieces. She felt like she had stepped back in time and the otherworldliness of her surroundings appealed to her. Her life was in transition, even as she transformed into a person of her own choosing. It seemed fitting that her new life should begin in a place so different from her past.

"It's all so beautiful," she said admiringly, unable to hide her excitement.

"Isn't it though?" Helen looked up from where she was busily turning down the covers on the bed. "I've always loved the view from here. My rooms face that way, too. I've come to know the look of the sea in every season."

"Have you been here long?"

"Oh, goodness, yes. My family has been employed by the Yardleys for over forty years. I wasn't yet twenty when my husband and I came. This was just the summer house then, of course. We spent most of our time at the Philadelphia home. It's only since—well, I've been here for the last fourteen years."

"And Mr. Yardley lives here year round as well?"

Helen hesitated once again, then merely responded, "Yes."

Anna was eager for any information that would clarify the strange circumstances of her new job, but was reluctant to pry. The little housekeeper seemed just as reluctant to discuss the issue of Anna's employment. It might have seemed strange had it not been for the atmosphere of long-ago customs clinging to the place.

"What's in here?" Anna called, pointing to a door opposite the large bed.

"Your sitting rooms and bath." Helen pushed the door open, revealing a large room with a stone fireplace. French doors led out to a balcony, and several comfortable chairs and tables formed a sitting area before the hearth. A modern bath adjoined the room.

"It's wonderful," Anna exclaimed. "I never expected anything like this."

She tried to temper her enthusiasm, reminding herself she might not be staying. She realized how much she had been counting on this position, and how comfortable she already felt.

"Are your rooms like this?" she asked, trying to disguise her worry. *What am I going to do if I have to leave?*

"The very same," Helen exclaimed. "Now, I'll leave you to get settled. You'll have to bring your own bags up, though. I'm afraid there's no butler. Tea will be at four in the library. I'll come to take you down then."

"I really should wait to unpack until I speak with Mr. Yardley. I might not be staying."

"Posh," Helen replied, giving Anna a quick hug. "Of course you'll be staying."

Anna hoped that Graham Yardley agreed.

CHAPTER TWO

Just make yourself comfortable in here, dear," Helen said as she showed Anna into a large room filled with floor to ceiling bookcases and fine leather furniture. Helen lit a fire in the huge stone fireplace. The evenings by the sea were cool despite the deceptive warmth of the waning afternoon sun. "Graham will join you soon."

When Helen left to prepare the tea, refusing all help from Anna, Anna examined her surroundings. An oil portrait above the fireplace caught her eye. Anna recognized the bluff below Yardley she had seen from her upstairs window. In the painting, a lone figure stood on an outcropping of stone, one arm draped over a bent knee, commanding the vista of sea and sky. Deep black hair, wild and windblown, framed a face in profile marked by chiseled features and piercing dark eyes. A flowing black great coat nearly obscured the figure, open only enough to expose a ruffled white shirt, tailored trousers, and black boots. A pair of black leather gloves, clasped loosely in one hand, completed the picture of the lord of the manor. It was an image from another time, brooding and untamed. Anna was surprised to see by the date that it was done only fifteen years before. Anna imagined this was Mr. Yardley, and he certainly appeared to be all that the master of such an estate should. Aristocratic, handsome, and austere. She supposed she would soon discover that for herself.

Anna pulled a small footstool in front of one of the large chairs in the central seating area. She extended her legs toward the warmth of the fire and leaned back, watching the crackling flames, wondering if she wouldn't soon be headed back to Boston. She was nearly asleep when a deep voice behind her startled her from her reverie.

"Miss Reid?"

Anna turned, stifling a gasp of surprise as she found herself face to face with the figure in the portrait. Standing before her was one of the most striking women Anna had ever seen. Her portrait, however arresting, had not done her justice. She was quite tall, with thick black hair brushed back from an exquisitely sculpted face. Her eyes, perhaps her most compelling feature, were nearly black, as the artist had depicted, and contrasted sharply with her pale, luminescent complexion. The oils however had not conveyed the intensity of her gaze, nor the glacial severity of her bearing. Anna tried not to flinch at the scar which marred the handsome face, running from just below her hairline across the broad forehead to one elegantly arched brow.

Anna stared, completely at a loss as the woman approached. The dark-haired woman leaned slightly on an ornate walking stick, and, despite a slight limp, was imposing in finely tailored black trousers and an open-collared white silk shirt. A gold ring with some sort of crest adorned the long fingered hand that she held out to Anna.

"I am Graham Yardley," the woman stated simply. It was delivered in a tone that left no doubt as to who was the master of Yardley Manor.

Anna rose quickly, grasping the outstretched hand. She was instantly struck by the delicacy of the fingers that held hers briefly. She cleared her throat, which felt suddenly dry, and answered, "How do you do? I'm Anna Reid."

"Sit down, please," Graham said somewhat tersely, turning toward the chair facing Anna's. Anna, still a little stunned, was about to sit when she heard a noise at the door.

"Graham! Be careful!" Helen cried.

Even as Helen called a warning, Graham stumbled over the small footstool in her path and lost her balance. She reached out, muttering an oath, struggling not to fall. Instinctively, Anna grasped her about the waist, surprised at the willowy strength in Graham's reed-slender form. Anna steadied the taller woman against her, aware of the rapid pounding of Graham's heart.

"Are you all right?" Anna cried in alarm. She could feel her shaking.

Graham pulled away sharply, her dark eyes furious, her body rigid with tension. She steadied herself, her hand nearly white as she clenched her walking stick.

"Helen! How did that footstool get there?" Graham demanded angrily.

"It was my fault. I moved it," Anna said quickly, alarmed more by her employer's physical distress than her anger. The woman was still trembling, though she was trying hard to hide it. "I'm sorry." She looked from Helen to Graham in confusion. Graham drew a shaky breath, struggling for composure.

Suddenly, with horrifying clarity, Anna realized that Graham Yardley was blind. That realization brought a quick flood of sympathy, and she said without thinking, "Oh God, I'm so sorry. I didn't know."

"How could you know?" Graham rejoined roughly, reaching behind her with one hand to find the armchair. She lowered herself slowly, her expression betraying none of her discomfiture. She would not be humiliated further by enduring empty condolences. "There is no need to dwell on it. Be seated."

Helen came quickly to her side, watching Graham with concern. She extended a hand as if to touch her, then quickly drew back. "I've put the tea in its usual place. Will you need anything else?"

"No. Leave us."

As Helen stepped away, Graham held up her hand, her voice softening. "It's fine, Helen. You needn't worry. On second thought, could you bring us some sherry?"

As she spoke, Anna could see her host relax with effort against the cushions. Her face lost its edge as well, reflecting the unexpected gentleness of her tone. Anna found her expressive features captivating— as well as quite beautiful.

Helen smiled tenderly. "I'll get it right away."

They sat in silence as Helen brought glasses and poured the sherry. She handed Anna a glass and left Graham's on the small table near her right hand. The silence continued for a few moments after the housekeeper pulled the heavy library doors closed behind her. When Graham reached for the glass and raised it to her lips, her hand was steady again.

"Forgive me," she began in her deep mellifluous voice, "I haven't asked if your accommodations are suitable."

"The rooms are wonderful," Anna replied. "The view of the sea is exquisite." Instantly she regretted her remark, but Graham merely nodded, a distant look on her face.

"I know. I always stayed in that room when I was a child."

Anna willed herself to be calm and tasted the sherry. It felt warm and comforting as she swallowed. She couldn't stop staring at the woman across from her. Her mere physical presence was imposing, defined less by gender than by the pure elements of beauty and elegance, much as a classical sculpture is often androgynous at first glance. She was aristocratic, her every movement refined. She was scrupulously polite and obviously used to being in charge. She was aloof, remote, unapproachable. She was more than a little intimidating.

"Did Mr. Norcross explain what your duties are to be?" Graham continued, unaware of Anna's discomfort.

"Not in detail. I'm afraid I may not be what you're looking for. I have no experience managing a household."

"Really?" Graham remarked dryly, raising an eyebrow. "Mr. Norcross led me to believe that you had been married and now live independently. That sounds as if you have managed at least two."

Anna laughed a little grimly. "Neither was much of a challenge, I'm afraid. Certainly not on the scale of Yardley Manor. I worked to help support my husband through law school, and since my divorce I've been a graduate student."

Somehow, much of the story seemed like someone else's to her now. Looking back on the last ten years of her life, Anna felt as if she had been sleepwalking through her days. When just out of college, she had married a man who shared the same values as she and who seemed to have the same vision for the future. Anna had a degree in botany that she couldn't use, so she worked part-time in a florist shop while Rob was a student. Eventually, they accumulated all the material trappings of a successful young couple of the eighties, including a renovated brownstone in a gentrified area of the Back Bay, a new BMW for Rob, and a Jeep for Anna. Anna had financial security, the correct circle of literate female friends, and an adequate, if not particularly exciting, love life.

Rob was content and Anna was bored. As Rob worked longer and longer hours to keep pace with the other young attorneys in his firm, Anna found herself with less and less to do. They had a maid twice a week and every modern convenience available. Neither of them had been eager for children, so Anna couldn't even mingle comfortably with the women of their social set who spent much of their time on the Commons with their strollers and their offspring. The frequent obligatory office socials became more of a burden than a diversion, and she and her husband grew steadily apart.

Anna shook off the memories, struggling to be honest with her would-be employer about her qualifications, or to be more honest, her lack of them, but needing desperately to find a way to make it work. "Can you tell me what it is that you require?"

Graham sighed slightly, turning toward the fire. In profile signs of fatigue lined her face, and Anna caught glimpses of gray streaking her dark hair. Anna guessed her to be ten years her senior, but despite her commanding tone and rigid control, Anna sensed a weariness that had nothing to do with the years.

"I need—assistance—with handling correspondence, reviewing accounts, running the day-to-day affairs of the estate. Helen cannot handle all of this any longer, and I—cannot do it alone. I have never had anyone else do it, and I don't want Helen to think that I've lost confidence in her. It has simply become too much. You would also have to do some rather menial chores, I'm afraid. Helen no longer drives, and it is difficult getting deliveries out here." She stopped, making an impatient gesture with one graceful hand. "We need someone at Yardley, it seems, who can manage in the world beyond our gates."

Her tone was bitter, and Anna could only imagine how hard it must be for a woman of such obvious independence to admit she needed a stranger to assist her.

"Ms. Yardley—"

"Please, call me Graham," Graham interrupted. "Everyone always has. It was my mother's family name, and to hear my father tell the story, I looked so much like my mother's father the name was never in doubt." She smiled slightly, and Anna caught a fleeting glimpse of her haunting beauty. When she gave expression to her feelings, breaking the aura of restraint, she was even more intriguing.

"Graham," Anna began quietly, "I am in something of a desperate situation myself. I want to continue in graduate school full-time. Without this job, I won't be able to afford to do that—not and keep a roof over my head, too. I'm afraid I'll need some help, but I would like to try this very much." She meant every word, and her sincerity showed in her voice. She didn't add how drawn she was to Yardley the moment she saw it, or how right it felt to be here. She couldn't admit even to herself how much the woman before her captured her imagination, and her curiosity. She very much wanted to learn more of Yardley, and its compelling master.

Graham ran a hand through her hair, leaving it tousled, and sighed again.

"It seems we are both in need of some assistance, then. Shall we agree to try it for a month or two?"

Anna smiled in relief. "I'd like that very much."

Graham nodded once, rose swiftly, and crossed to the door with deliberate steps. "I'll send for you when I need you. Good evening."

With that she was gone, her footsteps echoing in the quiet house. Anna sat for a moment, replaying the strange encounter. She was left only with impressions—fleeting glimpses of strength, and loneliness, and stubborn determination. And underneath it all, pain. Anna glanced up at the portrait, wishing it could reveal Graham Yardley's secrets.

Chapter Three

Anna spent her first evening at Yardley carrying the rest of her belongings upstairs, unpacking, and getting settled. Helen kindly brought her a tray with sandwiches and tea because she was too preoccupied with lingering thoughts of Graham Yardley to remember dinner. Then she was restless and couldn't sleep, so she curled up in a chair in her sitting room to read. She must have dozed for it was quite late when she was startled awake by a noise outside in the hall. She listened intently for a few moments, thinking she heard footsteps pause before her door. But then there was only the gentle creak of the shutters in the wind. Smiling to herself, she got ready for bed. As she lay awake, waiting for sleep to come, she mused again over her first meeting with her new employer. Rarely had anyone caught her attention quite so dramatically. Graham Yardley was impossible to describe in ordinary terms. Anna was quite sure she had never met anyone like her. As she drifted off to sleep, the image of the dark-haired aristocrat lingered in her mind.

She awoke very early the next day, as much from excitement as from the strangeness of a new house. It would take a little time to get used to the night noises of the old structure, the rhythmic pounding of the surf, and the absence of city traffic below her window. The quiet seclusion of Yardley Manor had truly transported her to a new world.

Shaking herself to dispel the last vestiges of sleep, Anna pushed back the heavy comforter and reached for a tee shirt. She moved quickly across the chilly room to the window, anxious for her first glimpse of Yardley in the morning. Looking down across the lawns, she was surprised to see a figure at the edge of the bluff, facing out toward the ocean. She recognized instantly the tall, slender figure of Graham Yardley. As the sun rose it struck her face, outlining her chiseled profile in stark relief against the sky. Standing so still, her hair windblown, one hand clasping the ebony walking stick, she appeared hauntingly alone.

As Graham began to make her way carefully up the steep slope to the house, Anna stepped back from the window. She didn't want her employer to see her watching. Almost instantaneously she remembered that Graham could not see her. The fact of Graham's blindness saddened her deeply. She wondered why that should be, since she scarcely knew her. Perhaps it was the poorly concealed pain in her voice or the fierce pride beneath the tightly controlled surface. But more than that, Anna was moved by Graham's apparent isolation from the world. To Anna, that was the greatest tragedy of all.

She experienced life as a feast, enjoying it with all her senses. She loved to feel the spring sun on her skin, and smell the fresh turned earth, and taste the faint salt of sea air. And always, most of all, watching the colors of the world slowly cycling through the seasons. It was that love of life that drew her to the miracle of growing things and motivated her desire to design living spaces where people could exist in harmony with nature. The environment was the canvas of Anna's dreams. It troubled her unaccountably to think that Graham Yardley had withdrawn from that. Anna looked down into the ruins of the Yardley estate, imagining the beauty that once existed there, and she longed to know it as it had once been—flowering with new growth, rich with the pageantry of life.

She turned to dress with a sigh, reminding herself that the reasons this solitary woman chose to live secluded here by the sea were no concern of hers. What did concern her was that she had work to do, although exactly what that work was to be, she wasn't quite certain she yet understood.

When she entered the kitchen, she found Helen busy baking. The clock over the large oven showed the time as 6:20.

"My goodness," Anna exclaimed, "what time did you get up?" Helen smiled up at her as she placed biscuits on a tray to cool.

"Five o'clock. I can't seem to sleep late, no matter what. Old habits die hard, I guess. When all of the family was about, I'd have breakfast ready and the table in the dining room set by now. Mr. Yardley was a banker, and he always worked here after breakfast for a few hours before he left for town. He said he couldn't work without my breakfast. Thomas, that was my husband, was the general caretaker. He managed the grounds and oversaw most of the staff. He's been gone almost twenty years. My son worked here too before he went off to college. He's a doctor now. Lives in California. Even though everyone is gone, I still stick to my old routines." She pushed wisps of gray hair back from her face and straightened her apron. "How did you sleep?"

"Wonderfully," Anna said, eyeing the biscuits appreciatively. She realized she was starving.

Helen caught her look and laughed. "Have one. I'll have the rest ready in a minute. I was just taking a tray to Graham."

"Oh, won't she be joining us?" Anna asked, strangely disappointed.

"She's in the music room. She takes all her meals in there," Helen informed her, a fleeting expression of concern crossing her face. "She's been up for hours, I imagine. I'm not sure when she sleeps."

"How did she lose her sight?" Anna dared ask.

Undisguised pain fleetingly crossed the older woman's features. "A car accident."

She looked as if she might say more, but then quickly busied herself at the stove again. Anna regarded her silently. Helen obviously cared for Graham a great deal. Anna wished there were some way to ask Helen more about her solitary employer, but she knew instinctively that Helen would never discuss anything of Graham's personal life with her. It was clear that Helen guarded Graham's privacy as carefully as did the woman herself. She remained silent, although her questions multiplied with every passing hour.

After a sumptuous meal of biscuits, eggs and country ham, Anna insisted on helping Helen straighten the kitchen. As they worked, she said, "You'll have to give me some idea of how I can help, Helen. I want to be useful."

Helen nodded. "I know this all must seem strange for you. Graham told me that you were a student and would need time for your studies. I've made a list of things we need, but it shouldn't take too much time."

"Oh, don't worry about that," Anna said with a laugh. She was touched that both Helen and Graham had expressed concerns that she have time for her own work. "I was married for nine years, and I don't think that my husband once considered my schedule when he needed something done."

"Yes, well," Helen rejoined, wiping her hands on her apron, "they do tend to think that what they're about is the only thing that matters."

"To be fair," Anna sighed, "it wasn't all his fault. It took years for me to realize that both of us had changed, and that we wanted different things. We worked at it for a while, but in the end, divorce seemed like the best solution."

"It's hard, I imagine," Helen said sympathetically, "even when it's for the best."

Anna nodded, thinking that at thirty-two, she had ended up with a used Jeep, a third floor walk-up in the student enclave near Boston University, and a microwave oven she had rarely used. By the end of her first year of graduate school in landscape design, the proceeds from her divorce settlement had been nearly exhausted. Whatever she might have to do at Yardley Manor to make this job a success, she would gladly do.

"So," she said with determination, "let me see that list of yours."

It was only ten a.m. when Anna returned and began unloading the Jeep. It was a clear April morning, the air crisp and fresh. She felt wonderful and hummed as she climbed the steps to the kitchen. A bag of groceries in each arm, she called as she went, "Hello. Helen, I'm back."

She was surprised when Graham pushed the door open. She was wearing an immaculately tailored pale broadcloth shirt tucked into loose fitting gray gabardine trousers, somehow managing to look casual and elegant at the same time. Anna recognized the understated quality of her attire, the fit so perfect she must have all her clothing made for her. Despite her informal dress, Graham was the image of sophistication.

"Hello," Anna called softly, wondering why this woman made her feel so shy.

"Good morning," Graham replied, sliding the door back while Anna carried the bags to the counter. Graham stood listening for a moment, then to Anna's surprise said, "Let me help you."

Anna started to protest, then quickly stopped herself. She had gleaned from their brief meeting how critical Graham's independence was to her. Any suggestion that maneuvering the steps with packages in her arms might be dangerous would certainly provoke that formidable temper. "Of course. My Jeep is parked just to the right of the steps. The tailgate is down."

Graham nodded and started down the stairs. Anna watched her, noting that her slight limp was hardly noticeable this morning. Graham moved cautiously but confidently forward, her left hand lightly trailing along the side of the vehicle. When she reached the rear, she looked upward at Anna, who was still standing on the porch.

"Since you're here, why don't you hand me something to carry in?"

"Of course," Anna said, blushing as she realized she had been staring. Why did it seem like Graham knew that? She hurried to pull a box from the Jeep. She handed it to Graham, who cradled it against her chest. Anna didn't move until she saw Graham up the steps safely and through the door. Then she grabbed up the last of the bags and rushed inside. She found Graham emptying the carton onto the long counter top. Now and then Graham would turn an object over and over in her hands, her long fingers exploring the shape. Anna was fascinated by the delicate movement and caught herself once again staring at her enigmatic employer.

"Olive oil," Anna said when Graham frowned over the bottle in her hands. "I think I buy that brand because I love the shape of the bottle."

Graham nodded, caressing the curves of glass, committing the shape to memory. "Sensuous, isn't it?" she remarked quietly, as if speaking aloud without realizing it.

Anna blushed for no reason she could understand. "I never thought of it that way, but you're right."

Graham set the heavy bottle down abruptly and straightened her back, her face suddenly remote.

"When you're done here, I'd like you to join me in my study. It's the last room on the right."

"I'll be there in a minute," Anna replied as Graham quickly left the room. She sorted the rest of the parcels, then poured a cup of coffee from the pot Helen had left steeping on the stove. As she headed down the hall, she tried not to think about the fact that it wasn't the bottle she had found so sensuous, but the intimate way those graceful hands had held it.

Chapter Four

Anna knocked at the partially closed door of Graham's study. "Come," Graham called, her deep voice sounding distracted. Anna's attention was immediately drawn to a magnificent grand piano that stood before double French doors. The doors were open to an enormous flagstone patio. It was the same terrace above the slope to the sea cliffs that Anna had first seen from her bedroom windows. Opposite the piano was another fireplace and sitting area. Graham's breakfast tray lay on a small table beside several large leather chairs. She sat at a large walnut desk, stacks of papers and envelopes piled before her. Sunlight streamed into the room, highlighting the angular planes of her face.

"What a lovely room," Anna exclaimed.

Graham raised her head, a slight smile softening her features. "Isn't it? Soon, the roses at the edge of the terrace will nearly obscure the view."

Anna glanced at her in surprise before remembering that Graham hadn't always been blind. *How sad, never to see the roses bloom again.* She blinked away sudden tears. Perhaps it was that unexpected emotion, or the appreciation she heard in Graham's voice, or the sight of the rose bed Graham remembered, now nearly obliterated by wild growth, that prompted her to speak impulsively.

"You know," she began hesitantly, "the grounds are badly in need of attention. All the gardens are overgrown—many of the paths are nearly gone. They are literally choking to death. The house is suffering from weathering and could use repair, too."

Graham's face was remote. "I hadn't realized. We haven't had a gardener here in years," she added absently, unwillingly remembering Yardley in another life. She forced her thoughts back to the present, crushing the memories. "Perhaps you could look into it. Make any arrangements you think necessary."

Anna adopted her employer's formal tone, afraid that she had given offense. "I will, thank you. I'll keep you informed, of course."

Graham waved her hand dismissively, her mind clearly elsewhere. "I thought we might go through some of this correspondence. It's been neglected for months."

Anna took a seat beside the desk, availing herself of the opportunity to study her employer. Close to her now in the light of day, she could see the fine lines around her eyes and the abundant gray streaking her coal black hair. The scar on her forehead scarcely detracted from the symmetrical arch of her full, dark brows, the high cheekbones or the strong chin. Her lips were soft and full, in striking contrast to the stark planes of her face. Her eyes were dark and clear, and although Anna knew them to be sightless, the gaze that fell upon her was penetrating nevertheless.

"Why don't we begin with these," Graham said, indicating a stack of unopened envelopes by her left hand. "If you could read them to me, I'll tell you which ones need a reply. There's a tape recorder there for you to make notes."

For the next hour they sorted mail into piles, some to be discarded, some to be forwarded to Graham's attorney, and some that needed Graham's personal attention. Anna was surprised at the scope of Graham's financial involvements, and a little overwhelmed.

"You know, some of this is quite beyond me," she said at length. "You need more than someone who can barely balance her own checkbook."

Graham stretched her long legs, leaned back in the leather desk chair, and shrugged, apparently unconcerned. "Never mind. You'll learn." She stood and walked to the open doors. Leaning into the breeze, her hands in the pockets of her trousers, she turned her face up to the sun. Anna observed her with interest, trying to imagine how one experienced a world one couldn't see.

"It's nearly one o'clock, isn't it?" Graham said at length.

Anna glanced at her watch. "A few minutes before."

Graham nodded, crossing to the long buffet on the opposite side of the room. She reached into a small refrigerator enclosed within and withdrew a bottle.

"Would you like some champagne? It seems a reward for our efforts would be appropriate."

Anna smiled. "I'd love some."

Anna watched intently as Graham confidently set two crystal glasses on a silver tray, opened the bottle, and placed it carefully in an ice bucket. Turning to Anna, she held out the engraved silver tray.

"If you could take this, we can sit on the terrace. If you don't mind the slight chill to the air," Graham added, raising a questioning eyebrow.

Reaching for the tray, Anna smiled. "I'd rather be outside no matter what the temperature."

"Very good," Graham remarked, apparently pleased.

She followed Graham across the flagstone terrace to a round wrought-iron table near the ornate open stone balustrade. A sea breeze blew up from the ocean, ruffling Graham's hair. Graham faced the water, a slight frown on her face.

"Are you quite sure you're not cold?"

"I'm wearing a sweater," Anna replied softly, moved by Graham's thoughtfulness. Graham herself was more exposed in her thin cotton shirt. "Can I get you something warmer?"

Graham took a seat next to the glass-topped table and shook her head. "It doesn't seem to bother me."

Graham slid her hand across the table to the tray, deftly found the glasses, and expertly poured their champagne.

"Thank you," Anna said, accepting the glass. Graham nodded slightly in response, and together they turned toward the sea. Silently they basked in the spring sun, not quite warm yet, but full of promise. Anna found herself surprisingly content in the presence of her austere employer. Despite her reserve, Graham displayed moments of warmth and quick humor that were quite engaging.

"Graham," Anna began at last, "I'd like to see what I can do with the gardens. There is so much beauty here, and it needs care. I'd enjoy doing it myself."

Graham's expression was guarded. "David Norcross told me that you are a landscaper. Tell me about it."

Anna sketched her history for Graham, passing quickly over her marriage to describe the last year of her life. She explained her classes and found herself revealing her hopes of some day having her own business.

"You mean to be more than a gardener, then," Graham commented seriously.

Anna laughed. "I love the physical work, but I also want to be involved in the actual design."

"You'll need help with Yardley. There was a time when we employed two gardeners here full-time."

Anna nodded. "And you'll need to hire someone again. But I can handle the formal gardens myself."

"But if I understood you correctly, you have your own work to do," Graham protested. "My work alone, never mind Helen's needs, will keep you busy enough. It would seem that undertaking to save Yardley too would be quite a task." Although her tone was lightly mocking, her face was quite serious.

Anna was strangely touched that Graham gave any thought to her work, let alone considered it important. What a surprise this woman was.

"I don't need to go to school this summer—in fact, I can really use the break. And, besides, working here at Yardley will give me a chance to practice some of my ideas. There's so much that needs to be done. I promise, if I can't handle it, I'll be the first to say so."

Graham spoke softly, her voice dreamlike. "You can't imagine how lovely Yardley was in the spring. There were blossoms everywhere, new life, bursting from the earth. I would walk for hours through the gardens, just looking at the colors. The spectrum of hues in the sunlight was like a symphony for the eyes. I couldn't wait to get here—out of the city, away from the crowds. After a long tour we—" She stopped abruptly, a quicksilver flash of pain passing across her face. The hand that held the fine crystal flute tightened. Anna feared for a moment that Graham would break it in her hand.

Anna tried to imagine what it would be like knowing she would never see another spring. Saddened, she felt an uncommon tenderness for this woman who had lost so much. Impulsively, she said, "You'll know when the roses bloom. You'll be able to smell the blossoms in the air."

"Yes." Graham saw no reason to explain that she rarely walked about during the day. At night, in the dark, it didn't matter that she couldn't see. She would not have to imagine what she was missing in the sunlight. Impatiently she shook her head. She thought she was long past such regrets. "Do what you like. If you find that you need help, hire someone. I've arranged a household account at the bank in your name."

"Oh, no. You hardly know me."

"I know what I need to know." Graham rose abruptly, suddenly anxious to be done with this conversation. She did not want to remember—any of it. "I'd like to see you tomorrow at one o'clock. We can continue with the papers then."

Anna stared after her as Graham disappeared into the house. She wondered how Graham would spend her time until next they met. Each time she saw her, she was left with more questions and greater curiosity about her enigmatic host.

Chapter Five

Anna stretched her back, cramped from the long hours in one position. She surveyed her progress. Graham was right—she was going to need help. Nevertheless, she was happy with the start she had made in the gardens below the terrace. In two weeks she had pruned back the rose bushes and bordering shrubs, and had rescued most of the perennials from the thick vines that had encroached upon them over the years. Since her mornings had quickly become filled with managing the affairs of the house, she worked mostly from mid-afternoon until dusk. The Yardley household itself required little attention. Whatever needs Helen had were easily accomplished on Anna's trips into the city for her classes. However, Graham owned property in both Boston and Philadelphia. Much of the financial matters were directed to the attorneys, but Anna found herself becoming quite adept at dealing with building managers, contractors, and accountants over the phone.

Several times a week, she assisted Graham with her business affairs, a task she had come to enjoy. From their afternoon meetings, Anna was slowly gaining an impression of Graham's many dimensions, despite her carefully guarded exterior. Anna found her to be impatiently dismissive of any and all financial matters, despite the fact that she was clearly wealthy. If engaged in quiet conversation she was attentive, gracious and altogether charming. However, when forced to confront the affairs of the estate she made decisions quickly, occasionally displayed flashes of temper when annoyed, and seemed altogether uninterested in the practical issues that occupied most people. Whatever captured Graham's mind when she suddenly fell quiet, her attention clearly eclipsed by some internal voice, Anna sensed it had nothing to do with the world she herself was familiar with.

Despite the fact that they spent several hours together nearly every day, Anna still knew so little of her. Graham easily drew Anna into discussions of her life, but she never spoke of her own past. Anna became more and more intrigued as the days passed. She wondered what thoughts, and more importantly, what feelings, lay hidden beneath the silent inscrutable features.

Anna sighed and tossed her trowel into the toolbox. Despite her fatigue, the hard physical labor satisfied her. Her days were full, and she was coming to view Yardley as her home. She looked forward to breakfast and dinner with Helen, only wishing that Graham would join them. Each evening, Helen took a tray to the music room before serving their own meal. After she and Helen cleaned up together, Anna retired to her rooms, often falling asleep before the fireplace. She never saw Graham in the evening, and she came to realize that she missed her formidable presence.

She carried her tools around to the gardener's shed in the rear of the property. As she passed by the terrace, the notes of a haunting melody carried out to her—soft, and gently flowing, but so incredibly sad. The doors to Graham's music room stood open, the lace curtains wafting out on the late afternoon breeze. Glancing in, Anna was surprised to see Graham seated at the piano. It was the first time she had ever seen her playing. Without thinking, she drew nearer, captured by the beautiful music. Standing before the open doors, she watched Graham as she played. This was a Graham she had never seen.

Her eyes were nearly closed, and as her body moved commandingly over the keys, her face reflected the essence of the music. She was lost in the melancholy notes, critically alone.

Anna's throat constricted as she watched and listened, knowing with certainty that at that moment, Graham Yardley and her music were one. She remained unmoving until Graham finished, then stepped softly away. The image of Graham, staring sightlessly down at her hands on the silent ivory keys, remained etched indelibly in her mind.

"Graham asked that you join her in the music room when you're free," Helen called to her as she passed through the kitchen.

"Yes, thanks," Anna replied absently, still disquieted by the scene she had just witnessed, unable to say exactly why. She showered quickly and was soon knocking on the closed doors of Graham's study.

"We need to deal with some of the personal correspondence," Graham said perfunctorily when Anna joined her. "We have been getting too many calls lately."

"Certainly," Anna answered, instantly alerted by Graham's tone that something was disturbing her. She wished she could ask her what troubled her, but Graham's unapproachable demeanor prevented even that simple inquiry. Ignoring her disquiet, she crossed to her usual seat at the desk and began to peruse the letters Graham had obviously ignored for months. Anna was amazed at the scope of the solicitations. She began to read aloud at random, for all the letters were similar in theme.

"These two conservatories have written several times in the last two years requesting that you teach a master's class," Anna informed Graham, who had begun pacing soon after Anna began reading messages to her. Anna had never seen her so agitated before.

"Tell them no," Graham replied curtly, her face grim.

"There are a number of inquiries regarding your concert availability," Anna said quietly, subdued by the well-known companies seeking to engage Graham as a guest performer.

"Throw them away," Graham said flatly. She stood with her back to Anna in the open terrace doorway, and the hand she rested against the frame was tightly clenched.

"There's a graduate student at Julliard—she's written and called several times. She says she's writing her doctoral thesis on your early works—" Anna faltered as Graham caught her breath sharply. "She would like to arrange a meeting with you, and perhaps discuss your current—" Anna was stunned to silence as Graham whirled toward her, a furious expression on her face.

"Don't make me repeat myself!" she snapped. "I *don't* perform, I *don't* compose, and I don't give goddamned *interviews*. Go through whatever's there and deal with it. I don't want to hear anything more about it!"

Anna stared as Graham searched for her walking stick with a trembling hand. She had never seen Graham misplace anything in her surroundings before. It was heart wrenching to see her falter uncertainly as she tried to orient herself.

"It's against your chair," Anna said quietly. She looked away, giving Graham time to compose herself. She knew Graham could not see her, but it seemed wrong somehow to witness her private struggles.

"Graham," she ventured tentatively, not wanting to add to Graham's obvious distress, but unable to ignore what she had read. "These things look important. I can't just throw them away. I don't think I can answer them without your help."

Graham paused at the door, her back to Anna, rigid with her struggle for control. "I've given you my answer to all of them, Miss Reid—no. Word it any way you want, but handle them yourself in the future. That's what I'm paying you for. Don't bring them up to me again."

Anna risked Graham's ire with one last attempt. "If you could just give me some idea—"

"Enough, Anna," Graham said wearily as she pushed open the heavy door to the hall. "It's done."

Anna was more than curious; she was shocked, both by what she had read as well as by Graham's reactions. She had very little exposure to formal music, but even she could appreciate from the nature of the requests that Graham was no ordinary musician. The magnitude of Graham's response was even more bewildering. Anna wanted very much to understand what had just happened, but she could not ask Graham. Anna knew Graham well enough by now to know she would never discuss something so obviously personal, let alone something that caused her such anguish. Her pain was clearly evident, but Anna sensed that Graham would never admit to it. It was the nearly palpable intensity of that pain more than anything else that propelled her from the room in search of Helen. She found her sewing in the library.

"We need to talk, Helen," Anna said gravely as she joined the older woman in the seating area.

Helen regarded her first with surprise, then, at the sight of Anna's distress, with apprehension. "What is it?"

"It's Graham," Anna replied. "Tell me who she is."

"Oh, my goodness," Helen pronounced, "that would be quite a task. I've known Graham since she was just a baby. Mrs. Yardley died when Graham was only three, and I guess I became the closest thing she ever had to a mother. Lord, forgive me, but I think I love her more than my own flesh and blood. I wouldn't know where to begin."

Anna was beginning to expect Helen's evasions whenever Graham was the subject, but she was too shaken by the strange scene with Graham to accept more non-answers. It was enough that Graham shut her out with her unimpeachable graciousness and impenetrable emotional barriers.

"Start with these," Anna demanded, holding up a fistful of envelopes. "Carnegie Institute, Paris Conservatory, London Philharmonic—and a dozen others. You should have seen what these did to her. She's suffering, and you *know* she won't admit that, let alone explain it. I'm supposed to be here to assist her. I can't be of any help to her if *both* of you keep me in the dark."

Helen regarded her solemnly, a lifetime of guarding Graham's privacy warring with her concern for Graham's well being. In the end she finally conceded that Graham needed someone's help, and Anna cared enough to ask. She decided the time had come for one of them to trust someone. She set her sewing carefully aside and crossed to the library shelves. She took down several heavy leather bound books and handed them to Anna.

"I think this is what you're asking about."

Anna opened the cover of the first volume to find press clippings, articles, and reviews, all of them about Graham. The earliest dated back over thirty years. With an increasing sense of wonder, she studied the chronicle of Graham's life.

Graham Yardley had first come to the attention of the music world when she was only six years old. By then she had studied the piano for three years. The young music teacher her father first employed soon recognized that the headstrong young child was advancing far too rapidly for normal instruction. An interview was arranged with a renowned instructor at the Curtis Institute, who accepted the little girl as a pupil. By six she was giving recitals, by her teens she had appeared as a guest soloist with a number of internationally prominent orchestras, and by twenty she had won not only the Tchaikovsky competition, but every prestigious music contest on every continent. She had been lauded for her innovative interpretations of classical works, as well as for her own compositions. Her talent seemingly knew no bounds.

The decade of her twenties was a time of intense international touring and performances. The London Times, the Paris Review, the Tokyo press and dozens of others celebrated her as the next heir to Rubenstein and Horowitz. There didn't seem to be enough superlatives to describe her. Seemingly she had not yet reached her peak when the coverage simply stopped. Anna was left with a void, staring at empty pages, desperately seeking some further glimpse of the great pianist all the world had welcomed.

"My God, Helen," she murmured, closing the books gently, swallowing the urge to cry. Laying them aside, she met Helen's questioning gaze. Just as she knew Helen was waiting for her to comment, she knew that her response would determine what else Helen might share. In the end, all she could do was speak from her heart.

"She's really quite special, isn't she?"

Helen smiled softly. "It's strange that you should say that—I always thought of her that way—special. People who didn't know her thought her genius came easily. I knew that whatever she was born with, the music she made came from her heart's blood. When she was working, you couldn't drag her away from the piano. For days and nights on end she'd go without sleeping. I'd practically have to force myself into the room with a tray of food. She'd be pacing or playing, struggling with some refrain. When she'd finally come out—'starving', she'd say—she would be so happy. I knew she loved it; you could feel her excitement when she had gotten it just right."

Helen paused, searching for words to portray a personality that by its very uniqueness defied simple description. The icon the world had worshipped was merely the public image of the complex, complicated, and all too human woman Helen had known.

"She's been called so many things. A gifted child prodigy they said when she was six, a remarkable composer they said when she was twenty, and at thirty they called her a master. Some things they said aren't written down in those articles. There were those who called her arrogant, temperamental, an egotistical perfectionist. All those things were true, but she was so much more to those who knew her. Whatever she demanded of others, she demanded ten times that from herself. She put all of herself into everything she did, and expected the same from others. She was the force that drove all of us, and in return she gave us beauty beyond belief. We made allowances I suppose, for her temper and her arrogance. She was never cruel or malicious, simply so intense, so consumed by her music. She was the light of our lives."

Anna sat quietly, trying to imagine Graham like that, wishing she had known her. When she thought of the tormented, anguished woman who would not even hear of the world she had once ruled, Anna's heart ached. Where was that imperious virtuoso now?

"What happened to her, Helen?"

"The accident changed everything," Helen said with a finality that warned Anna not to probe for details.

"Helen," Anna began tentatively, "I heard Graham playing today. It was so beautiful. Why doesn't she perform any longer?"

Helen shook her head. "She won't play for anyone anymore. Hasn't since the accident. She was in the hospital for months. When she was finally released, she came immediately to Yardley. She's lived here ever since. Her father was alive back then, of course—it's been over ten years. He stayed on at the main house in Philadelphia, and I came here to be with Graham. He visited, but I knew it was hard for him to see her so changed. At first friends would call, and so many important people from the music world, but she wouldn't see them. For months she barely spoke or left her room. After a while, she began to go outside, mostly at night. She wouldn't let me help her. She's always been so stubborn, even as a little girl." Helen smiled at some memory. "It broke my heart to see her stumble. Sometimes she fell, and it was all I could do not to run out to her. But, oh such pride. I knew it would hurt her more if she knew I could see her like that."

It was physically painful for Anna to imagine what Graham had suffered, or the extent of her loss. Neither could she imagine that the stubborn independent woman she was coming to know would simply give up.

"But, Helen. She's still so strong. What's happened to her?"

"She didn't go near the piano for that whole first year, and I feared for her mind, I really did. I can never remember Graham without her music. When at last she began to play again, I thought everything would be all right. But the music was so sad. I don't care about that anymore. I'm just happy that she plays at all."

"It doesn't make sense. She can manage quite well, and with a little help—"

Helen looked alarmed. "Oh no, my dear. It's not because of her injuries. I only wish it were. Graham lost something much more than her sight in that accident. She hasn't composed a piece of music since she came home from the hospital. It's as if the music left her that night—after she had lost so much already."

"But what—" Anna began, confused.

Helen stood suddenly, gathering her things. "I've gone on too long, I'm afraid. I must sound like a silly old woman to you."

"Oh, Helen. I know better. It must have been so hard for you all these years."

Helen smiled. "To have Graham home, alive, was all I wanted. If only I could see her happy again. I wish you could have known her—so accomplished, so full of life. She loved her music so, and the world loved her. When she toured, the concert halls would be full. People stood for hours to hear her play. Oh, she was something to see—like a young lion, so graceful and proud."

"She still is, you know," Anna said softly. "I heard her play, I *felt* her music—it was one of the most powerful things I've ever experienced."

Helen looked at Anna strangely. "You can see it, then?"

"Oh, yes," Anna exclaimed. "She has such passion—in her hands, in her voice—even in those beautiful eyes."

Helen touched Anna's face tenderly, then turned quickly away. "I think it will be good for us that you have come."

When Anna found herself awake and restless at midnight, she returned to the library. She curled up in the large leather chair, books open in her lap, compelled to revisit Graham's past. She searched the newspaper and magazine images of the vigorous artist, struck by her vitality and fierce passion. The photos of Graham on stage, lost in the rhapsody of her music, were among the most arresting portraits Anna had ever seen. Anna was stirred as if by the memory of one she had once known and now missed. There was a sense of loss that felt deeply personal. As Anna lay tossing later that night, searching for sleep, the strains of Graham's music echoed in her mind.

CHAPTER SIX

Reluctantly, Anna conceded to Graham's wishes. When more than a week had passed with no further overtures from Graham to address her personal correspondence, Anna wrote replies. Since she had no specific instructions, she simply stated that Ms. Yardley appreciated the inquiries but was not presently available. She could neither bring herself to leave the letters unanswered nor to close the door on Graham's previous life. It was too final and felt much too much like death. Graham's death.

It was beyond tragic to accept that the Graham Yardley she had glimpsed in the yellowing pages of history was gone forever. Anna could not accept it, not when she heard Graham walk the halls late into the night, or awoke to the sight of her outlined against the dawn at the cliffs' edge. Not when she heard those melancholy chords waft on the breeze in the darkest part of the night. Stubbornly Anna clung to the hope that Graham herself had abandoned, the hope that the music would someday return to Yardley.

Time passed, and frustrated that she could not help Graham, Anna worked instead to restore Graham's home. Summer was approaching, and Anna had taken the task to heart. She hired carpenters and painters to work both outside and in, tending to the multitude of small details that had been neglected for a decade. She finally relented and hired a landscaping crew that she had seen advertised in the university paper. They would be helping her to clear the wide expanse of nearly wild growth that covered the rear slopes and the bluff above the sea.

When Anna walked down to the sea cliffs where Graham stood nearly every morning at dawn, she was terrified to find the path almost totally obscured with roots and vines. She couldn't imagine how Graham had avoided injury all this time. To make matters worse, the sea wall was crumbling into the surf a hundred feet below. There was precious little safety in that spot, especially for a woman who could not see. Anna knew it would be useless to ask Graham not to go there. Anna could envision the reaction that would produce. And, in truth, Anna didn't have the heart to bring it up. Whatever compelled Graham to visit that desolate point of land morning after morning didn't matter. Anna couldn't ask her to give up one more thing in her life. She simply hired a contractor and had the stone abutment repaired.

Yardley was alive with activity, and Anna was everywhere, supervising, directing, working to keep her mind occupied and free of her nagging worry about Yardley's master. People were always about, but she made it clear to the various workers that Graham's music room was not to be violated.

Graham was vaguely aware of the commotion, but avoided the bustle as much as she could. She neither questioned nor commented on Anna's undertakings, sensing that Yardley was safe in Anna's capable hands. It was a late May morning when Graham entered her music room and immediately felt another's presence. She stood still just inside the door, head cocked, listening, trying to discern the unexpected visitor. Then, she knew.

"Anna?" she inquired with faint surprise.

"Yes," Anna answered uncertainly. She was standing with her back to the door and hadn't realized Graham was there until she spoke. She hadn't expected Graham at all. She was rarely about during the morning.

"What is it that you're doing?" Graham asked as she crossed the room. Her voice wasn't critical, merely curious.

"I'm putting a vase of flowers on the mantle. I just picked them," she replied quietly. She was well aware that she had not been invited into Graham's study, but neither had Graham told her she was not welcome to go anywhere in the house she desired.

"To what purpose?" Graham asked darkly. "Did you think I might enjoy the color?" She didn't want reminders of what she could no longer see.

Anna caught her breath as Graham stalked to the French doors, flinging them open to stand in the archway, her back to Anna. Bright sunlight streamed around her, but she was in shadow, a stranger to the day.

"I thought you might enjoy the beauty of their scent. I only wish that you might enjoy the sight of them as well." Her voice quivered with both anger and uncertainty. She didn't want to hurt her, but she couldn't stand to see her deny all that remained to her. She stared at the rigid back, not realizing she was holding her breath, wondering if she had pushed this volatile, wounded woman too far. She waited for the hot flare of temper.

Graham drew a long steadying breath. "Forgive me," she said quietly. "That was unconscionably rude of me. Please accept my apology."

"I didn't mean to upset you," Anna replied. "You needn't apologize."

"I thought I could smell the roses on the wind last night," Graham said softly, her back still to Anna. The rigid stance relaxed, to be replaced by a weariness too often evident in her whip-slender frame.

Anna approached her cautiously, afraid Graham might retreat if startled. "Yes, they're in bloom again now. They've been waiting so long."

"Have they?" Graham questioned, her gaze fixed on some distant point beyond the open terrace doors. "I would have thought they had simply perished by now."

"Their roots are deep, and strong," Anna said softly, wondering if they still spoke of the flowers. "The soil of Yardley is rich and fertile; it has nourished them all this time."

Graham stood very still, aware that Anna was close beside her. The air about them was filled with the perfume of new life. It was the first time in years she could recall smelling the spring fragrances.

"Nourishment alone is not always enough. Living things need more than that. They would not have survived indefinitely without care," Graham said softly.

"No," Anna replied, swallowing the ache in her throat, "but they didn't have to." Impulsively, Anna grasped Graham's arm. "Walk with me—I'll show you."

Graham tensed at the first touch of Anna's hand upon her arm. The sensation was so foreign it startled her. Then, with the grace born of her breeding, she tucked Anna's hand in the bend of her elbow. "All right," she agreed, allowing Anna to lead the way. As they strolled the meandering paths, Anna stopped frequently to describe the young flowers, drawing Graham's hand to the soft buds.

"Daffodils?" Graham asked as Anna brought a petal to her face.

Anna smiled. "Yes—wait," she said, plucking another blossom. "And this?"

Graham cupped her fingers around Anna's hand, bending her head over the flower nestled there. Softly, she inhaled. "Wisteria?" She looked up to Anna expectantly.

Anna stared into the questioning eyes, struck once more by their expressiveness. For an instant, she was certain that Graham could see her. She would give anything to make it so.

Graham felt Anna's hand tremble slightly in hers. "Anna?"

Anna released the breath she hadn't realized she was holding. "You're very good. Right again," she said, her voice thick with an emotion she couldn't name.

Graham slipped the blossom from Anna's grasp and tucked it into the pocket of her shirt.

The simple gesture touched Anna. It pleased her unaccountably to bring the gardens to life for Graham. Each smile that passed Graham's lips, however fleeting, was a gift. Oddly, she was even enjoying their physical closeness. Even though Graham could maneuver the garden paths perfectly well, she made no move to remove the hand that Anna kept on her arm. Anna found herself curiously aware of the muscles rippling under her fingers as they walked. She forced herself to pay attention to the uneven terrain, trying to ignore the unusual fluttering in her stomach.

Graham stopped suddenly, a puzzled look on her face. She turned to her right and stretched out her hand. "Where are the lilacs?"

Anna was startled that Graham should know. Graham's ability to orient herself in her environment continued to astound her.

"You're right, of course. They're here, but they were so badly overgrown that they haven't flowered in years. I cut them back. In a year or two they'll flower again."

Graham leaned on her walking stick and sighed. So much was gone. "I'm sorry. They were always so lovely. They were my favorites, I think, after the roses."

Anna placed her hand over Graham's, whispering, "They'll be back."

Graham shook her head, her expression once again dark. "There are some things, Anna, that once lost, simply cannot be restored. There is no use in struggling to reclaim them. That path leads only to greater disappointment."

"I cannot accept that," Anna insisted. "One must hope." Graham remained silent as they made their way to the house. She knew only too well that with the passage of time, even hope would die.

Helen carried a tray into the music room as she did each evening, placing it on the table beside Graham. Tonight, Graham seemed lost in thought. She held a flower in her hand, tracing the petals absently with a fingertip. As Helen turned to leave, Graham called to her.

"Helen?"

"Yes, dear?"

"Sit a moment, won't you?"

Surprised by the unusual request, Helen sat anxiously waiting. Although she and Graham spoke often, their conversations were always casual. Graham never discussed her deepest thoughts, and never sought Helen's advice. Even as a child she tended to make announcements about her intentions, such as the time she informed her father she wasn't going back to regular school. She never did.

She had been eight.

"Would you like some champagne?" Graham asked as she filled her glass from the bottle by her side.

"Oh goodness, no—you know how silly I get when I drink that."

Graham smiled. "You just talk a little more. But you're never silly."

Helen leaned to touch Graham's arm gently. "Is everything all right, dear? Is there something we need to talk about?"

"Anna," Graham replied after a moment. "Do you think she's happy here? It must be very lonely for a young woman so far away from the city, with no friends nearby."

Helen had known Graham since the day she was born. She had seen her through great triumph and greater tragedy. She had watched her lock her heart and mind and talent away in the empty rooms of this desolate house for a dozen years. This was the first time in all those years that Graham had mentioned another person, let alone noticed someone enough to question their happiness. Anna's presence had penetrated

Graham's self-imposed isolation, and that was close to a miracle. Helen chose her words with care. "She seems to love it here, Graham. Why, I can hardly remember what it was like before she came."

Graham made an impatient gesture. "Nor I. But that's not the point. Yardley is our home—we chose this place, this life, you and I. Anna didn't. We mustn't take advantage of her kindness, or her—caring."

Helen thought she had an inkling of what really concerned Graham. Anna was an unusual woman. She appreciated Graham's notoriety, had understood her fame, and yet she was not overwhelmed by it. In Graham's entire life, there had been very few who had ever dared approach her with friendship. Her imposing personality and public stature prevented ordinary relationships. People were either afraid of her intensity, or her temper—or they wanted something from her. She had had many followers, and many would-be friends, but it was rare that anyone tried to know her. Graham's personal attachments had most often been the source of her greatest disappointments. After all these years alone, she would surely distrust any type of intimacy.

"Graham, Anna is a grown woman. And she's made a lot of hard decisions in her life. Leaving a marriage is hard, even when it's not a good one, and I imagine striking out on her own without much security was hard, too. But, she is strong and independent, and she knows what she's about. She's here because she wants to be, and if she becomes unhappy, I imagine she'll do something about that herself. I don't think there's anything to worry about."

Graham relaxed perceptibly. "Helen?"

"Yes, dear?"

"What does she look like?"

Helen could only imagine what a difficult question that was for Graham to ask. Graham knew the description of every piece of clothing in her closet, and insisted that each item be returned from the cleaners in a certain order. She never asked for assistance in dressing, never asked for help if she needed something to eat, never asked for any help at all. The only concession she made to her lack of sight was the necessity of keeping the furniture in one place. For her to make a direct reference to her inability to see was unheard of.

"Oh, Lord, that is a hard one," Helen exclaimed, nonplused.

Graham rose impatiently, reaching a hand up to the mantle, her face turned toward the fire. "I know that she is almost my height, and strong. I could feel that in her hands when she took my arm in the garden. She laughs softly when something pleases her, and she loves the land. She knew how to bring the flowers to my mind's eye—" She halted in frustration, unable to complete the picture of the woman who was so often near, but whom she could not see.

"You already know the best parts of her, Graham—her goodness, and warmth, and her wonderful love of life."

Graham turned around, her fists tight. "Yes, but what does she *look* like? What color is her hair? Her eyes? What does she wear? Helen, I can't see her."

Helen longed to go to her, to stroke the anger and frustration away. She knew very well that Graham would not allow it, would not allow any sign of sympathy.

"Her hair is blonde, rather like honey, and cut back away from her face. Her eyes are very blue, like the ocean on an August morning. When she's excited about something, her skin flushes a light rose and her eyes sparkle. In my day, we'd call her wholesome. She has the kind of strong body women have these days—you can tell she's fit, but, she flows in the right places, too."

"How long is her hair? What colors does she wear?"

"Her hair just touches her collar, and it's not so much curly as wavy. It blows around in the wind, like yours does, all wild and free. When she's working outside she sometimes ties it back with a bandanna round her forehead. She likes to wear those loose trousers with the drawstrings at the waist, and tee shirts—or those men's shirts that are made for girls. Lovely colors—purples, dark greens, deep golds."

Graham had become very still as Helen talked. The tension slowly left her body.

"Does that help?" Helen asked her.

Graham nodded, concentrating on the picture forming in her mind.

"She's not at all like Christine, is she?" Graham asked softly.

"Oh my dear, not a bit."

Anna waited impatiently in the kitchen. Helen had been gone for so long. She had been starving when she came in for dinner, but the longer Helen was absent, the more anxious she became. Graham had been so subdued on their way back to the house that Anna was certain something was wrong.

"Is Graham all right?" she asked the moment Helen rejoined her.

Helen looked at her in surprise. What had gotten into the two of them? They were both so jumpy. "Yes, dear, she's fine. She just wanted to talk to me about a few household things. Now, why don't we eat before everything is completely cold."

Forcing herself to relax, Anna poured them each some coffee and joined Helen at the kitchen table. She tried to appear nonchalant.

"I was just a little concerned. She spends so much time alone, and she's so very sensitive—"

"That's her nature," Helen commented. "All she ever wanted was to play the piano. Her father had to force her to do anything else. He adored her, though. I thought he would go mad himself after the accident. For so long we didn't know if she would live, and then when she finally opened her eyes, he was sitting right there by her bed. She put out her hand to take his. She didn't say anything for the longest time; we didn't know that anything was wrong. It did break his heart when she said, so quietly, that she couldn't see him. Oh, it was a horrible time."

Anna closed her eyes with the pain of the image, of Graham so brutally injured, of a family so hurt. Some part of her longed to change the past, to undue the horrible suffering.

As if sensing her thoughts, Helen said, "We all felt so helpless." She shook herself, rising briskly. "It doesn't change things, does it, to wish for the past to be different?"

"What was she like, before the accident?" Anna asked quietly.

As each day passed she wanted to know more. She was certain that the key to Graham's silence and her pain was hidden in her past. Anna couldn't stop thinking that if she could only understand what had caused Graham to withdraw from all she had been, she would find some way to reach her. Exactly why that mattered so much to her she couldn't put into words, but she knew she had never been so affected by anyone in her life. Maybe it was just knowing what an incredible genius Graham Yardley possessed, and that the loss of such a gift went beyond personal tragedy.

Helen laughed. "She was a regular hellion—she never got on well in regular schools. Not that she wasn't bright—she was always good at whatever she tried. It's just that she never wanted to do anything except play the piano. She said once that when she looked at the world, she heard music. It was her language, as natural to her as talking is to us. All you ever had to do was listen to her play to know what she was feeling. It's the one place she could never hide. When her father put her in the music school, with tutors at home, she did much better. From the time she was young she was in the company of adults, and she never had a childhood. She had been all over the world by the time she was fifteen. She grew up surrounded by people who wanted things from her—a piece of her fame, a piece of her passion. Her music might have been pure, but the world it thrust her into wasn't. Sometimes I feared it would destroy her." Helen sighed. "She loved a good party, though, and, oh, what a good dancer. She made up for all the hours she spent lost in her work by being a little wild. But we all forgave her for the times she worried us, because she was such a wonder. She brought us all so much happiness."

Anna tried to imagine Graham that way, infused with energy and enthusiasm. That there were great depths to her sensitivity, Anna had no doubt. But Graham's passionate embrace of life had disappeared. What Anna couldn't explain was her own desire to rekindle it.

CHAPTER SEVEN

Anna respected Graham's wishes and did not mention the abundant correspondence that still arrived regarding her former career. Graham remained for the most part an easy person to work for, and if it weren't for the fact that Anna was acutely aware of Graham's deep unhappiness, she would have found Graham's company more than satisfying. On those occasions when they escaped from the drudgery of paperwork to relax on the terrace, Graham seemed sincerely interested in Anna's life. Anna enjoyed their times together, only wishing for some way to make Graham's rare smile linger.

Unexpectedly at first, Graham began to appear in the garden while Anna was working. She would stand nearby, often wordless for long lengths of time, and then simply disappear. Eventually she started to ask Anna what it was that she was doing. Graham would listen attentively, then smile to herself as she made a mental note of a new shrub or planting. She was slowly creating a new vision of Yardley with Anna's help. As the days passed, her visits became more frequent. Anna found herself looking forward to these encounters. On those days when Graham didn't appear, Anna finished her work strangely restless and unsatisfied.

Late one morning Anna glanced up to find Graham close by. Her hands were thrust into the front pockets of her trousers, and she leaned forward with a perplexed expression on her face.

"What are you wondering?" Anna asked, leaning back to see her tall companion.

"What you're planting. This isn't the rose garden, or the English garden, or the perennial bed—in fact, this isn't anything at all as I recall." Graham gestured toward each of the gardens as she spoke.

"You're right on all counts. This is the kitchen garden."

Graham frowned. "We don't have a kitchen garden. Helen always said she couldn't grow weeds, and I—I never had the time." Her expression became distant, a response Anna was coming to recognize. Whatever the memory, it was painful.

Anna reached into her carry all. "Here," she said, placing a pair of soft work gloves into Graham's hand. "Put these on." Graham turned the gloves over in her hands, clearly at a loss. Anna found her consternation appealing. She was usually so commanding. Had she known her bewilderment was apparent, Anna knew Graham would have been embarrassed.

"But why?"

"So you can help plant the tomatoes," Anna said matter-of-factly. "We're making a garden so we can grow our own vegetables this summer." She knew she was risking alienating her reclusive employer, just when she seemed to be emerging from her isolation, but she had to try. The gardens seemed to bring Graham some peace. Anna only hoped her instincts were correct. She was quite sure that no one had ever suggested to Graham Yardley that she dig in the dirt.

Graham hefted the gloves. "I don't need these."

Anna studied Graham's hands. They were long-fingered and delicate, ribboned with fine blue veins beneath soft pale skin. The supple fingers suggested strength, but they were not meant for rough work. Anna had seen Graham's hands on the keyboard, how they moved with certainty and grace. She had heard the music from those hands on the night breeze. She did not need newspaper accolades to know they were exquisite instruments in themselves.

"You do need them," Anna said softly. "Please put them on. I can't let you do this without them."

Graham hesitated for a moment, then nodded. She slipped them on, then asked, "Where do you want me?"

Anna grasped her sleeve. "Here, on my right. Give me your hand." She placed a seedling in Graham's palm. "There are twelve of these in each flat. Make a hole six inches deep, then put the seedling in, pot and all. Press the earth firmly around the peat pot, so there are no air pockets. Put the plants a foot and a half apart. Move straight to your right back toward the house. All right?"

Graham brought the young plant to her face. It smelled like warm sunshine. For a moment she was lost in the comfort of it.

Anna watched the transformation of her elegant features. Graham cradled the tiny plant reverently, her face losing its stark tension, relaxing into a gentle smile. The tenderness she hid so well was plainly evident now. Abruptly Graham emerged from her reverie, and with a shake of her head, her expression was once again inscrutable.

"I can do that," she said with her usual confidence. With utter disregard for what must be five hundred dollar trousers, she knelt beside Anna as directed.

"Good," Anna replied. She watched Graham work for a while, amazed at her self-assurance and dexterity. She also noted the care with which Graham handled the delicate new life. She was a wealth of contradictions—remote, emotionally distant, intimidating, and yet she showed such tenderness and sensitivity in the small gestures that she didn't realize were so revealing. Anna found it hard to take her eyes off her. Eventually she forced herself back to work, and the time passed in companionable silence. As the sun climbed above them, Graham paused to roll up the sleeves on her shirt. She leaned back and Anna caught a glimpse of her face.

"Graham," Anna called, "turn towards me." Graham swiveled around, a questioning look on her face. "Oh hell. You're burning!" Anna cried in consternation. She hadn't thought the sun was that strong, but then it occurred to her that part of Graham's pallor was from her rare time outside. She knew Graham walked the grounds late into the night. Only recently had she begun to venture out during the day. Anna grabbed a tube of sunscreen and knelt by Graham's side. "Put this on your face—and your arms, too."

"Are you sure?" Graham questioned reluctantly.

"Of course I'm sure," Anna exclaimed, angry at her own carelessness. "You should see how red you are." The instant the words were spoken, she wanted them back. "Oh, God! I'm sorry."

Graham opened the tube. "Well, I'm not. I know what I look like with a sunburn."

Anna thought she looked more striking than ever with color in her face. "It's not that bad, but if it gets any worse, I think Helen will kill me."

"Better now?" Graham asked as she covered her hands and face with the lotion. She lifted her head toward Anna for inspection. Her hair was windblown and tumbled over her forehead in disarray. Sunlight etched the angles of her face in gold, a dazzling contrast to the rich black of her hair and eyes. She was unknowingly stunning, and as Anna gazed at her something visceral shifted in her depths.

Shaken, not wanting it to show, Anna reached for the tube. "Here, give it to me," she said hoarsely.

She brushed the cream across Graham's jaw and down the side of her neck. "You missed a spot," she said softly, cupping Graham's chin gently in one hand. She sensed Graham struggling not to pull away and wondered why she was uncomfortable. Was it her blindness that made her so, or something else?

"Thank you," Graham remarked seriously when Anna took her hand away. The touch of Anna's fingers on her skin had startled her. Even Helen rarely touched her, and Graham had not thought she missed it. She had little need of contact with anything save the keys of her piano. Still, her breath caught in her throat at the sensation of Anna's fingers on her face. She struggled to control her expression, aware that she was trembling.

"You're welcome," Anna replied, moving away. She had a hard time forgetting the look on Graham's face when she innocently touched her. It looked like fear.

"Graham!" Helen cried when Graham walked into the kitchen. "Oh my gracious. Did you fall? Are you hurt?"

"I'm fine. Why?" Graham answered in surprise. She felt better than fine, in fact, she felt strangely exhilarated.

"Why, you've got dirt streaked on your face, and your shirt is a sight." Graham took meticulous care in dressing, and Helen could never remember her with so much as a crease out of line on her tailored trousers.

Graham frowned. "I was gardening—apparently rather messily. Just how bad do I look?"

When Helen got over her astonishment, she laughed with delight. God bless Anna for this. "I'm afraid you wouldn't like it. You look— disheveled."

Graham put down the glass she was about to fill. "I'm going to shower," she said stiffly. She left with as much dignity as she could.

Helen looked after her, tears of joy threatening to fall.

Graham was startled by a knock on the door of the master suite. Helen never disturbed her when she was in her rooms. She rose from the chair that faced the open windows, calling, "Yes?"

"Graham, it's Anna. I have something for you."

Graham opened the door to admit her, a question in her eyes. By way of explanation, Anna placed a package in her hands.

"These are for you," she said, suddenly shy. It had seemed like such a good idea when it first occurred to her. With Graham standing in front of her, as unassailable as always, she wasn't sure.

Graham motioned her inside with her usual grace. "Please, sit down."

Anna looked about, surprised by the luxury of Graham's quarters. Everything from the high four-poster bed to the ornate armoires and antique dressers spoke of cultured refinement. Graham projected such an austere impression that Anna had to remind herself that Graham had grown up in and been part of the very pinnacle of wealthy society. Her only visible concession to that opulent world now was her taste in clothes. Anna watched Graham carefully as she opened the parcel.

Graham stood by her bed, meticulously examining each item, her expression growing more and more perplexed. She said nothing as she carefully arranged the strange gifts. Finally she faced Anna, one elegant eyebrow arched in question.

"And these are?" she queried, her voice carefully uninflected.

Anna took a deep breath. "Two pairs of denim jeans, three blue cotton work shirts, six white cotton tee shirts, crew socks, and a pair of Timberline work boots."

"Interesting," Graham noted, struggling to keep her voice even. "And the purpose?"

"You can't garden in Seville Row suits and Italian loafers. It's criminal," Anna stated. She didn't add that it was also unsafe for Graham on the steep, often muddy slopes in the shoes she usually wore.

"I have never worn blue jeans in my life," was all Graham could think to say. No one had ever been so bold as to comment on anything she had ever worn before. In fact, such an attempt would have drawn her most scathing reply. That Anna had taken it upon herself to actually *buy* her clothing astounded her.

"They're black, not blue," Anna answered smartly. "I thought you'd prefer that."

"And how did you manage the size?" Graham asked, still strangely subdued. Anna was one of the few people she had ever known who did not seem intimidated by her. The other had been Christine, and that had been entirely different.

"I write out your checks," Anna explained. "I called your tailor."

Graham couldn't hide her shock. "You called Max Feinerman about *blue jeans?* What on earth did he say?"

Anna smiled at the memory. "He told me more than I'll ever need to know about your inseams, rise and waistbands. I had a hard time convincing him that it wasn't necessary for him to *make* the jeans, even though he insisted vehemently that he had always made all of your clothes. He's delightful." She didn't add that he also obviously adored Graham, and had asked anxiously when he might be needed to tailor her next concert suit. He explained her trousers were cut to allow easy movement on a piano bench and that since Graham had an unusually long arm span, she needed extra width in the back and sleeves of her shirts. It was important, he said, that nothing impair her reach on the keyboard. His pride in assisting Graham had not diminished during her years of seclusion. Anna was coming to realize that Graham made an indelible impression on everyone she touched.

Graham smiled softly as Anna spoke, one finger aimlessly tracing the cuff of her fine Irish linen shirt. "Poor Max," she said with a hint of laughter. "He probably hasn't yet recovered."

"Try them on," Anna suggested boldly.

Graham started with surprise, then laughed unexpectedly. "All right, Ms. Reid, I will. If you would be so kind as to excuse me for a moment." She gathered the clothes and disappeared into her dressing room, leaving Anna with the memory of her laughter.

CHAPTER EIGHT

Helen opened the music room door with one hand, Graham's breakfast tray balanced in the other. It was five a.m., and the sky visible through the open terrace doors was just beginning to lighten. It was the first of June, and although it was still cool in the early mornings, Graham had begun taking her meals outside on the stone patio. She was there at the edge of the balcony now, facing as always down to the sea. At the first sight of her Helen halted in astonishment.

"Graham?" she queried, her voice rising in surprise.

Graham turned, a distracted look on her face. "Yes? What is it?"

Helen collected herself quickly. "I—well, it's—you look quite nice."

Graham tilted her head, frowning. Helen wasn't making any sense. "I look—ah, the jeans. You've noticed the addition to my wardrobe. I'm not sure I'm used to them yet."

"Wherever did you get them?"

"Anna decided my day wear was not suitable," Graham answered.

"*Anna* bought those clothes?" Helen cried in amazement. No one in Helen's recollection had ever had the audacity to buy apparel for Graham. She was much too particular. That Anna was not only bold enough to do it, but that Graham seemed to have accepted the gesture with aplomb, amazed her.

"And do you approve?" Graham asked testily. She couldn't quite envision how she looked, and was irritated to discover that she cared.

Helen studied her in frank amazement. She was broad in the shoulders, with narrow hips, and naturally sinewy. The white cotton tee shirt highlighted the muscles of her chest and arms. The close fitting jeans accentuated her leanness and height, giving her a tense feline appearance. She looked ten years younger and tautly lithe. In all the years Helen had known her, her appearance had always been refined, dignified, and wholly elegant. She had a kind of natural androgyny that suited her professional persona. Graham as an individual was secondary to her role as a musician. Her gender on the concert stage was of little consequence. This was the first time Helen had ever had a sense of Graham as a sexual being. It was a disconcerting, and at the same time, wonderfully gratifying change.

"You look quite acceptable," Helen managed to say in a tone that belied her astonishment. She was afraid overt enthusiasm would make Graham self-conscious. She knew it would be hard for Graham not to know how she looked.

Graham nodded absently, recalling Anna's reaction when she had emerged from her dressing room. Anna was silent so long Graham began to think she had missed a button in some delicate location.

"Well," Graham had asked with a trace of impatience, "do they fit or shall we have to call Max?"

Anna had cleared her throat, saying, "The fit is fabulous. You look altogether—*handsome.*"

Handsome she had said. Graham wondered what Anna saw when she looked at her. She had never given it any thought before. How she appeared to others meant nothing to her. It had only been her music that mattered. Why it should matter now, when she had nothing to offer anyone, eluded her. And why she should care what Anna Reid thought of her was even more mystifying. She could not deny however, that she had enjoyed pulling on these clothes when she awoke that morning, and that as she did so, she remembered Anna's soft praise.

"Put the tray down, for heaven's sake, Helen," Graham said brusquely, annoyed with her own reminiscences. What did any of it matter?

When Helen returned an hour later, Graham was gone and her breakfast remained untouched.

Hours later, Graham walked down the garden path to the sea, vaguely aware of the fine salt mist against her skin, absently welcoming the sun's warmth on her face. She had been preoccupied since she awoke that morning. The hint of a refrain trailed in and out of her consciousness, making it impossible for her to concentrate on anything else. The notes were elusive, but ever present, and that was an experience she hadn't had in years. Whereas once music came to her unbidden, demanding expression, that inner voice had been silenced along with the surging rhythms of her once vital life. Why it should return now, she didn't know, and she was afraid to question it, lest the music desert her once again. She was feeling the notes, searching for the form, when she struck something large and unyielding in her path. She had no time to react, tumbling forward, emitting a curse as she found herself lying tangled in a thicket by the side of the path.

"Damn!" she swore, struggling to free herself from grasping tendrils of ivy.

"Oh my God, Graham!" Anna cried, rushing to her. "Oh God, are you hurt?" She began frantically pulling at the vines, attempting to pull Graham upright. *Please don't let her be hurt!*

Graham took firm hold of Anna's hands, stilling her frantic motion. "I'm quite all right. Just take my arm and help me up." Anna reached for her hand and slipped her other arm around Graham's waist. She was surprised once again by the strength in the deceptively lithe body. She gasped when her worried eyes searched Graham's face. "Oh Lord, you've cut yourself," she cried. With trembling fingers she brushed a trickle of blood from Graham's chin.

"What was it?" Graham asked quietly, trying to regain some semblance of dignity.

Anna looked devastated. "My wheelbarrow. How could I have been so careless?" She was close to tears. "God, you could have really been hurt."

Graham stared toward Anna. "Your wheelbarrow?"

"Yes," she said miserably. The thought of Graham injured was unbearable. She had begun to see Yardley as a maze of potential obstacles, all waiting for Graham to walk innocently into their midst. Every time she watched Graham maneuver the uneven flagstone path, or climb the crumbling steps from the bluff, her heart pounded with anxiety. Seeing her reach across the stove for the coffee pot, knowing how easily her sleeve could touch the flame, made Anna want to scream out loud. She cursed whatever godless force had stolen Graham's sight, and exiled this magnificent being from the world. That she might have been the cause of further harm completely undid her. She didn't seem to be able to think quite rationally where Graham was concerned. She held onto her protectively, one hand brushing at the smudges on her tee shirt.

Graham reached out for Anna's hand, laughing. "Was it a trap?"

Anna cradled the long, delicate fingers in hers, aware of how vulnerable Graham was despite her stubborn independence. "No, just my thoughtlessness," she managed around the tightness in her throat.

Graham was suddenly serious, aware of the trembling in Anna's voice. She grasped Anna's shoulders with both hands, looking intently into her face. "It's not the first time I've fallen," she said gently. "I'm quite fine, you know."

Anna stepped closer until there were only inches between them. "No, you're not. You have blood on your face and thistles in your hair."

Graham laughed again, a sound that warmed Anna's heart. "Well, for heaven's sake, get them out. Haven't I disgraced myself enough for one morning?"

Anna gently disentangled the wisps of vines from the thick, rich hair, whispering softly, "You couldn't be undignified if you tried. I don't know how, but you elevate jeans and a tee shirt to an art form." Her heart was still racing wildly, and she couldn't quite catch her breath. She was close enough to smell the faint cologne Graham wore. It seemed to flood her senses as the rest of the world receded from her consciousness. She was dimly aware of a faint pounding in her belly.

A faint smile flickered at the corners of Graham's mouth as she straightened her shoulders, her hands resting lightly on Anna's bare forearms. "Am I presentable now?"

"You're beautiful," Anna answered thickly. A pulse beat in Graham's neck, and for some unfathomable reason, Anna wanted to rest her fingers there. Maybe it was the fear invoked by Graham's recent fall; maybe it was the sorrow she couldn't dispel after reading the articles about Graham's previous life; maybe it was the soul wrenching sadness of the only music Graham ever played, alone in the dark. Something made her bold enough to brush her fingers gently through the disheveled hair on Graham's forehead, and stroke the satin skin of her cheek. She rested her hand against the ivory column of her neck, scarcely breathing, her vision narrowed until Graham was all she could see.

At the first light contact of Anna's tentative touch, Graham closed her eyes, a light shiver coursing through her. A faint flush colored her usually pale cheeks. Her words came slowly, with the same caution she used when crossing an unfamiliar room. "I can feel the salt from the sea and the warmth from the sun on your skin. You smell of the earth—rich, dark, vital. *You* are alive—and that is true beauty."

Anna felt each word, as she had felt Graham's music, in some deep part of herself she hadn't known existed. Without thinking, she slipped her arms around Graham's waist, resting her cheek against the thin cotton shirt, embracing her gently.

"Thank you," Anna whispered against Graham's shoulder.

Graham was acutely aware of Anna's heart beating against her, of the soft swell of Anna's breast against her chest, and the fine tremor in Anna's body. Graham shuddered slightly and stepped back gently, taking a deep breath.

"The stone bench—is it still there, under the sycamore?"

"Yes," Anna said quietly, sensing her withdrawal. She had to let her go, not understanding why it was so difficult.

"If you don't mind the company, I'd like to sit out here a while." Graham needed distance between them, but she could not bear to leave.

"I'd love the company," Anna said softly. "Do you know the way?"

Graham laughed. "I used to. Are there any strange obstacles in the path?"

"All clear." Anna followed Graham with her eyes as she made her way carefully but unerringly to the bench. Only when Anna saw her safely seated could she return to her work. Even then she glanced up every few moments just to look at her. She was delighted that Graham had accepted her gift of new clothes so magnanimously. Not only were they more practical, she looked terrific in them. As much as she loved the impeccably cut trousers and dress shirts Graham usually wore, this casual garb was unusually compelling. She could still vividly recall her shock when Graham had first appeared in them. Whereas before Graham's clothes accentuated her ethereal aloofness, these form-fitting casual shirts and pants emphasized her sinewy sensuality. Anna stared while something foreign erupted in her, and her heart began to trip over itself. When Graham asked for her opinion, she couldn't admit that what had come to mind was 'breathtaking'. But she *was*, in that aristocratic way of some women, and each time Anna saw her, she was more aware of just how physically attractive she found Graham to be. She had no reference for what she felt, but it was clearly undeniable.

She pulled roots and transplanted the day lilies that were multiplying in great abundance. Although there was silence between them, she was acutely aware of Graham's presence and was soothed by it. When she glanced up at one point, she was struck by the distant expression on Graham's face. She was used to Graham's lapses in attention, although she was more accustomed to their accompanying some painful memory. Today Graham appeared distracted, but not distressed. Her eloquent hands were moving on her outstretched thighs, delicately, but with purpose.

"Where are you?" Anna called quietly, laying her tools aside.

Graham smiled ruefully. "I'm trying to capture a refrain—not very successfully, I'm afraid. It's been plaguing me all day."

"Can you hear it?" Anna asked, aware that Graham had never once spoken to her of music. That she did so now, so casually, made Anna realize that Graham was not fully present.

"Almost. It's there, like a fine murmur in my ear, but I can't quite bring it into focus."

"Why don't you hum it?" Anna suggested, taking advantage of Graham's apparently mellow mood. "Maybe that will help."

Graham tilted her head, frowning slightly, "You won't mind the noise?"

Anna laughed. "Of course not. Go ahead." She smiled, turning back to her work, enjoying the deep, rich timbre of Graham's voice. Gradually she became aware of fragments of an enchanting melody and sat back on her heels to listen. Quietly, she laid her tools aside and watched Graham.

Graham sat with her eyes closed, suffused in sunlight. Anna wasn't quite sure which was more beautiful, the music or its composer. She did know she had never been quite so moved, nor quite so content simply to look at another human being. Graham quieted, fixing her gaze towards Anna. "You've stopped working."

"I'm listening," Anna confessed in a voice thick with emotion.

Graham leaned forward, her expression intent. "Do you like it?"

Anna went to her instinctively, kneeling by her side. She placed her hand lightly on Graham's thigh. She didn't know how to say what she felt—how the melody enchanted her, soothed her like a gentle caress—how gracefully the notes flowed around her. She wanted to say that Graham's music made her hurt somewhere inside; that she welcomed the hurt because she felt it so deeply she knew she was alive. Listening, she had wanted to cry, and dance, and hold someone she loved. "It's beautiful. I felt things, I *wanted* things—things that I've never known, just from listening to you. It's wonderful."

Graham was silent for a long time. Her gaze drifted beyond Anna, to another place, to another lifetime, when she was whole and her world was filled with music. She had thought then that her world was filled with love, too. She knew now she had been wrong. Anna's innocent response to those faltering notes, not even a fragment of what she once wrote in an instant, reminded her painfully of what she was no more.

Her fingertips just brushed Anna's hand where it lay on her leg. She looked to where she knew Anna knelt, willing herself to see her. When she couldn't, she lifted a hand to Anna's cheek. "I wondered if you could hear something of what I felt. I think you do. You have been kind in your praise. Thank you."

Anna remained motionless, concentrating on the feather light stroke of Graham's hand. Despite its gentleness, it affected her deeply. The sorrow in Graham's eyes, as they searched her face unseeing, touched her even more. Was there no way at all to ease her endless torment? She didn't realize her hands had moved to Graham's waist, or that she leaned into Graham's embrace as she struggled for some words to convey the emotions that threatened to choke her.

Graham felt the heat of Anna's body close against her own and sat back abruptly, letting her hand fall away, breaking their connection. "I think I'll go in now. You must have things to do, and I have other matters to attend to."

Anna stifled a protest; she was embarrassed by how much she wanted her to stay. Graham had already begun to make her way back toward the house by the time Anna collected herself. Anna looked after her, confused, and hurt. Had her pitifully inadequate attempts to describe her feelings about Graham's music offended her?

Whatever the cause of Graham's withdrawal, Anna returned to her work feeling lonely, a penetrating loneliness she had never before known.

CHAPTER NINE

The sun was nearly gone when Graham rounded the corner from the rose garden. She halted abruptly when she heard the kitchen door slam with a bang. Anna's angry voice carried to her clearly.

"Mr. Reynolds," Anna shouted, her voice cold with fury, "do you mind telling me what this is?"

He looked at the canister she held out to him, not particularly disturbed by her anger. With a disinterested shrug, he said, "It's a solvent—you spray it on—"

Anna interrupted him in a deadly tone. "What was it doing on the kitchen counter?"

"Guess I left it there when I used the phone." He stared at her, confused. She did seem to be a little irritated. "You did say I could use the phone." He gave her his best grin, the one that always worked with his wife.

"Yes, I did," she said with steely calm. "And I expressly told you that you were to leave no tools lying around, and that you were absolutely not to bring anything into the house." She caught her breath, trying to control her temper. "Is it caustic?"

"Well, you'd get a nasty burn if you sprayed yourself. But, it's clearly marked—anyone can see—"

"No, Mr. Reynolds—*not anyone*," Anna exploded. "You're fired. Send me a bill for what you've done so far." She turned and slammed back into the house. She was shaking, not with anger, but with fear.

She heard the door open and whirled to confront him. This was not open to discussion. But it was Graham instead who stood inside the door, her face grave.

"That isn't necessary, Anna," she said quietly.

Anna was too distraught for caution. She was still upset over Graham's fall that morning; she had been upset ever since Graham deserted her so precipitously; and she was sick over finding an open canister of toxic fluid in the kitchen where Graham insisted on preparing her own lunch. "Yes, it *is* necessary. That was dangerous."

"I am quite capable—"

"Yes, you are," Anna interrupted, her voice rising, vibrating with an effort to contain too many emotions. "You are amazingly capable. I am well aware that there isn't much that you can't do. But, damn it, Graham, you *can't* see. And there's no point in putting danger in your path. You're so stubborn and I would hate it so if anything happened to you." Her voice broke, but she just couldn't help it. She seemed to be on an emotional roller coaster lately. She was moody, and she never had been before. She woke up in the morning feeling in charge of the world, only to find herself depressed and listless by the afternoon. She hadn't felt this out of sorts in the middle of divorcing her husband. If something happened to Graham. To her horror she felt tears threatening.

From across the room, Graham felt her distress. "Anna," she soothed, reaching out to her, finding her shoulders. She gently cupped Anna's face with her hands, her expression intent. "Look at me."

Drawing a tremulous breath, Anna searched Graham's face.

"I am careful. I have learned to be. Fire him because he didn't follow your orders—fair enough. But don't let my blindness burden you with unnecessary fears. It is enough that I am a prisoner—at least, in some ways, I deserve it."

"No! You could never—oh, Graham, no!"

Graham stilled her with the fleeting touch of one finger to Anna's lips. "It doesn't matter now. It's done." She softly brushed the hair back from Anna's neck, allowing the thick strands to run slowly through her fingers, before dropping her hands. Quietly, she said, "There are things about me you do not know, Anna—things that some might say warrant my fate. There may be truth in that; I've stopped asking. Whatever the case, I can't have you become a victim of my past. You must live your life and not worry about mine. Promise me?"

Anna nodded, so affected by Graham's words that her head was pounding. "I'll try. I promise."

Graham seemed satisfied and stepped back. "Thank you."

"Graham," Anna called as Graham turned away, loathe for her to leave, "do you want to finish the accounts tonight?"

Graham shook her head. "No. I'll send for you when I'm ready."

Anna was oddly disappointed, and suddenly the evening ahead of her loomed long and empty. She waited all that interminably long day and the ones that followed for some word from Graham. None ever came.

By the time Helen entered the kitchen shortly after five a.m., Anna had made coffee, put bread in the oven, and was pacing restlessly in front of the window. She had barely slept and her nerves were completely frayed.

"What are you doing up so early?" Helen asked in surprise.

Turning abruptly, Anna asked urgently, "Helen, where is Graham? I haven't seen her in three days. I looked for her at the sea wall this morning and yesterday. She hasn't been there, or out to the gardens, and she hasn't sent for me. What is going on?"

Momentarily dismayed by Anna's distress, Helen quickly composed herself. She had been shielding Graham Yardley for a great many years. "Why, she's in the music room."

"The music room," Anna repeated stonily, trying to contain her temper. "I have never known her not to open the terrace doors when she's in there. Why now? What's happening?"

"She's perfectly all right," Helen insisted, although her face betrayed her uncertainty.

Anna struggled with impatience that verged on panic. "Is that why you brought back the dinner trays untouched for the last two nights? Because she's *all right*? Damn it, Helen. Tell me!"

Helen sagged slightly, abandoning her facade of disconcern. She sat heavily at the table, motioning for Anna to join her.

"She *is* in the music room, and she's working—she's composing—something she hasn't done since the accident. I'm not sure it's going well. It's been so long. I bring her the trays, but she sends them away untouched; she sends *me* away. I know she hasn't slept. It is starting to frighten me."

Anna looked at her disbelievingly. "I've been up to the terrace behind her study. She's not playing. The room is dark—" Anna sighed. "Of course it would be, wouldn't it? She doesn't need the light. It's sound proof, too, isn't it?"

"Yes, as long as the doors are closed," Helen affirmed. "I don't know if you can understand what this means, Anna. I'm not sure I do any longer. Graham hasn't attempted a new work since her injury. Oh, she's written fragments—those sad melodies she plays. But nothing of any complexity, and nothing that's ever affected her like this. I used to pray that she would work again, but now I'm not sure it's a good thing. If she can't—I'm not sure how much disappointment one soul can bear."

"Give me the breakfast tray," Anna said quietly.

"Oh, no, Graham wouldn't like that," Helen protested.

"Helen, I don't give a damn if Graham likes it or not! Are you going to stand by for the rest of your life and watch her die a little bit more each day?"

Helen couldn't hide her shock, and the harsh words shook her to her core. She stared at Anna, stricken.

"Oh my God, Helen," Anna cried, stricken herself. "I am so sorry." She passed a trembling hand across her face, drawing a shaky breath. "I can't begin to apologize. I don't know what I'm saying. I've been worried sick about her, and I just—please, can you forgive me?"

"It's all right, my dear. I can see that you're upset for her." She turned to prepare the tray. "Maybe if I hadn't given in to her so easily all these years," she said doubtfully.

"No, Helen," Anna said compassionately, agonizing over the words she had uttered in anger. "Graham is a formidable woman, and I doubt that you or anyone else could have changed her. My God, if you hadn't been here for her all this time, who knows how she would have survived."

Helen remained silent, thinking that Anna had done more to change Graham's life in three months than all of her own attention over the years. She knew Anna had spoken from a place of caring, and she was grateful at last for someone who wasn't willing to let Graham simply slip away. Everyone else who had supposedly loved her had either been too devastated by her tragedy or too weak to stand between Graham and her pain. Why Anna was willing to, she didn't know. For now she was just thankful that she did.

"Take this then," Helen said, offering the breakfast tray. "But be prepared. You haven't yet seen Graham when she's battling her demons. Her temper terrified most people."

Graham stood, shoulders slumped, before the fireplace, her arms folded along the mantle, her forehead resting against them. She stared down into the cold ashes, her spirit as desolate as the unseen remnants of a once brilliant flame. The back of her linen shirt was rumpled and sweat-stained. From across the room, Anna could see her trembling.

Graham waved a hand distractedly. "Just leave it, Helen."

"Not until you eat," Anna said as she placed the tray next to the untouched dinner left from the night before.

Graham turned in surprise. "Anna?"

"Yes," Anna replied, struggling for calm. Graham's face was creased with fatigue, she was unsteady on her feet, and she looked like she had lost five pounds when what she needed was to gain twenty. Her physical fragility was shocking. Anna had grown accustomed to the force and power of Graham's presence, and to be confronted so vividly with Graham's vulnerability frightened Anna more than she could have imagined. *My God, this is killing her*. The thought was so terrifying Anna clenched her fists to keep from crying out.

"Leave it, please," Graham repeated softly. She forced a smile, trying to hide her weariness and crossed the room to the piano. She ran a hand along its edge as if caressing it. "Then go. I've work to do."

Anna took a breath. "I want you to eat first."

Graham frowned, her body rigid with tension. "I will. Later."

"No. Now," Anna repeated, knowing she was on dangerous ground. She knew that no one dictated to Graham Yardley, and certainly not when she was in the midst of a creative fury. She steeled herself for the storm that finally arrived. Graham straightened to her full imposing height, her dark eyes flashing fire.

"I don't have time to argue with you, Anna, nor should I have to. I am still master of this house and, if I am correct, you work for me. Don't interfere in something you know nothing about."

"I know you can't work like this."

"You presume to speak of my work?" Graham shouted, slamming the piano lid down in frustration. "What do you know of my work? Could you even *begin* to recognize a great piece of music, let alone understand what it takes to create one? Do you have any idea who I—" Graham stopped abruptly, realizing what she was about to say. *Do you have any idea who I am?* "Oh, God," she gasped, turning away. Who was she now?

Anna would have preferred the anger to the agonizing uncertainty that she glimpsed as Graham turned from her. Helen had voiced what Graham obviously feared. *What if she can't?* "Of course I don't know what it takes. I can't even begin to fathom what it demands of you to create what you have. I *do* know who you are, Graham, and I know you can do this. But you've got to stop driving yourself this way. It's only making it harder."

Graham bowed her head, both arms braced on the wide expanse of the silent grand piano. "Please leave me, Anna," she said quietly, her despondency apparent.

"I can't," Anna said desperately. "Not like this."

Graham ran a hand through her disheveled hair. "I didn't know you were so stubborn."

"There's a lot you don't know about me," Anna said softly as she moved quickly to Graham's side, grasping her hand. "Come, sit down."

Graham allowed herself to be led to the chair. She was truly too tired to protest. She was ready to admit defeat, she should have known better than to try—but the music was still there, so close to her grasp. She leaned her head back with a groan.

"Do you want champagne?" Anna asked.

Graham laughed faintly. "Isn't it morning?"

"Yes, but for you, it's well past time for bed. You've been at this three days, Graham. You can't keep this up," Anna said reasonably, trying to hide her own deep fear.

"I can't stop now, Anna. Not yet," Graham said frantically. "I've been trying so hard to seize the music. I think I have it, and then it's gone." She dropped her head into both hands. "Perhaps I just can't do it anymore. Perhaps I am the fool."

Anna couldn't bear to hear the defeat in her voice. She had already lost so much.

"Graham, you're tired, you're driving yourself. Have something to eat. Rest a while. It will come."

Graham shook her head. "I can't. If I sleep now, I may lose it all." She was riding the thin edge of control, besieged with uncertainty, exhausted, and nearly broken.

Anna couldn't stand by and watch her suffer any longer. "Graham," she said gently, sliding onto the broad arm of the chair, encircling

Graham's shoulder with one protective arm. "You can't lose it. It's part of you. The music *is* you. I know that much from hearing you play."

She slipped a hand into Graham's thick hair, massaging the cramped muscles in her neck. Graham groaned again, leaning her head back into Anna's hands.

"That's not fair, but it feels so good," she murmured.

"Close your eyes," Anna whispered, a catch in her throat.

"Just for a second," Graham relented. She was so very tired.

Anna kept Graham in her arms long after she finally succumbed to sleep. Tenderly, Anna pushed the damp hair back from her forehead, wincing at the dark shadows under her eyes. Her skin seemed even paler, if possible. Anna felt a fierce desire to safeguard this delicate spirit. She continued to stroke her hair softly as she slept. She drifted, peaceful for the first time in days, with Graham secure in her arms.

When Graham stirred some time later, the first thing she felt was the body pressed to hers. She was lying in Anna's arms, her cheek against Anna's shoulder, and an arm encircling Anna's waist. The welcoming heat from the other woman's presence surprised her. She hadn't known the closeness of another human being, nor wanted it, for more years than she could remember. Anna's nearness stirred memories, in her body and her mind, that she would rather leave buried. She knew she must move away; she was beginning to respond in ways she could not control. Some awakening need, however, cried out for Anna's touch.

"Are you awake?" Anna queried softly, absently sliding her hand down Graham's neck to rest her fingers lightly against the soft skin left bare by the open collar of Graham's shirt. She attributed the fine shiver that coursed through Graham's frame to her lingering fatigue. "Graham?"

"Mmm," Graham murmured, struggling to hide her erratic breathing. All of her consciousness seemed to be focused on the spot where Anna's hand lay. "My headache is gone, and the music is still there." She didn't add that Anna's nearness was making it difficult to concentrate on the distant melody. For some reason it didn't seem quite as urgent right then. She even began to dare hope that the notes would not desert her.

"Ah," Anna smiled. "Some breakfast then, and that champagne."

"I want to work," Graham protested, struggling to rise. Anna stilled her with a gentle hand on her shoulder.

"*After* breakfast."

Graham shifted in the wide chair so that she was facing Anna, her expression revealing her frustration. Anna longed to smooth the wrinkles from her brow, but now that Graham was awake she was hesitant to touch her. Instead, she regarded her silently, surprised by the emotions just the sight of her stirred.

"What is it?" Graham asked at length, aware of the scrutiny.

"You have the most beautiful eyes," Anna whispered.

Graham blushed faintly. "The scar," she began hesitantly, "is it very bad?"

Anna traced the scar with her finger, at last giving in to her urge to stroke the lovely face. "No. I hardly think of it—except that it reminds me of how much you've been hurt. Then all I want is to undo those hurts. I would give anything to change what happened to you," she finished softly.

"Why?"

"I don't know, Graham," she answered, moved to honesty by the quiet intimacy they shared. "I only know that when I look at you, I want to know you—who you are, what you feel, what makes you happy— and I know that more than anything else, I don't want you to hurt." She laughed rather shakily. "I don't quite understand it, but I can tell you I feel it."

Anna's passionate admission moved Graham profoundly. She could not doubt her sincerity; she could hear the tears in her voice. Suddenly she was awash with conflicting needs. She could no longer ignore her intense response to Anna's touch; her legs were shaking and the blood pounded insistently through her pelvis. This was desire, and that very fact was frightening. Graham drew away slightly, her face once again expressionless.

"You are a very kind woman," she said softly.

Anna stared at her in confusion. *Kindness?* Whatever she felt for this woman, it was much more than kindness. She sensed Graham's withdrawal, just as she had that day in the garden. To be so close to her, and in the next moment to have that connection wrenched away, left her with an aching hollowness that was harder to endure than anything she had ever experienced.

"If I eat now, will you let me get back to work?" Graham asked, moving away.

"Of course," Anna answered bleakly. She could not argue when she didn't even understand her own feelings any longer.

CHAPTER TEN

Helen approached the study with some trepidation the next morning. Anna had been subdued the entire previous day after speaking with Graham. Her only comment had been, "She slept a bit and she said she would eat. If she doesn't, call me." She had taken herself off to the gardens then and worked ferociously all day. When Anna finally appeared in the kitchen well after dark, she sank into the chair, eyes already half-closed. Helen had to assure her that Graham's breakfast tray had come back empty before she could get her to eat anything herself. When Anna dragged herself off to bed, Helen thought for sure she saw tears on her cheeks. Helen was beginning to despair that both of them would make themselves sick. *Well, something surely has to be done*, she thought to herself as she wrapped soundly on Graham's door.

"Come."

Graham was standing at the open French doors, obviously weary, but smiling.

Helen smiled back with relief. "How are you, my dear girl?"

"I've finished, Helen! It's only a simple variation, but I've finished," she said with a note of wonder. "The first real work I've done in years."

"Oh, I'm so glad."

Graham's expression darkened. "Yes, well—I can't be sure it's any good. I never gave it any thought before. I never questioned my music, never. God, what arrogance to think I dare to compose anything now. Music, above all else, must be alive. How can I create anything that lives, while I, I merely exist."

"Oh, but Graham, you *are* alive."

"Am I? I've forgotten what it means to care about anything, Helen—about you, about myself, about—anyone. The sun doesn't

warm me, the salt air no longer stings, the touch of another's hand—"
Her voice faltered and she turned away. "My body has become my
prison, as surely as my blindness is my jailer. How can these hands
make music, when I am captive in this solitude?"

Helen responded instinctively to Graham's distress, sensing
rather than knowing what tormented her. Graham never complained
of loneliness before there was someone to remind her of another's
companionship. "It's Anna, isn't it? Something has happened."

Graham stiffened, her face inscrutable. "No, nothing," she said
sharply. "She pities me because she is kind. That's all."

Helen shook her head. "She *is* kind, you are right in that. But pity
you she does not. She is too strong a woman herself to expect that you
would need her pity."

"She doesn't know me," Graham said bitterly.

"Then let her know you. You mistake caring for pity, Graham. Let
her care about you."

"No. That is not possible," Graham responded angrily. "For God's
sake, Helen. You of all people should know that. Have you forgotten
who I am? Or have you merely forgotten what happens when I allow
someone to care? Would you wish that for me again?"

Helen shuddered at the angry words, crying, "How can I forget
what love cost you, Graham? I see the cost every time I look at you. But
it need not always be that way."

"Perhaps for me, it does," Graham said faintly, exhausted by too
many assaults on her body and her soul. "Perhaps for me there is no
other way."

Helen recognized the resignation in her face and wondered if it
wasn't too late after all for Graham Yardley to find peace.

It was another two days before Anna saw Graham again, two
interminable days spent trying not to wonder and worry about her
difficult employer. Two days in which she tried to concentrate on her own
life, only to find that Yardley, and its compelling master, had become a
large part of her life. She thought of Yardley as home, and Graham and
Helen as her family. She couldn't imagine not being there.

When Graham finally joined Anna on the terrace early one warm
afternoon, she greeted Anna cordially, but with obvious distance.
Graham did not inquire how she had passed her time, or ask of details

about Yardley's renovation, or question after the progress of the gardens. Their budding friendship seemed to have disappeared, and to Anna's deep regret, the woman who had walked among the flowers with her was gone.

Graham Yardley was as reserved, aloof, and unapproachable as she had been the day they met. Anna keenly missed the small intimacies they had come to share, aware only now of how much those moments with Graham had come to mean to her. Struggling with the crushing disappointment, she tried to accept that Graham wanted nothing more from her than simple secretarial assistance.

"There is a letter here for you," Anna said perfunctorily. "Would you like me to read it to you?"

Graham nodded, her attention obviously elsewhere. She had delayed as long as she could before joining Anna again, but at the first sound of her voice, the memory of her touch returned with exquisite intensity. She struggled not to show how much Anna's nearness affected her, but she could not control the quickening of her heart.

With a sigh, Anna removed a sheet of lilac-colored paper, covered in script. She began to read aloud:

My darling Graham,

Forgive me for not writing all this time, but you seemed never to want to hear from me. I've called many times, wishing to visit, but Helen always told me you would not see me. All these years you have never left my mind, even though I doubt you will believe that.

Anna faltered to a halt, uncomfortable with the intimate tone of the message. "This is very personal, Graham. Perhaps Helen should read it to you."

"Finish it," Graham ordered grimly, rising so quickly that her chair toppled to the flagstone surface of the patio. Muttering an oath, she righted it and began pacing along the edge of the balcony.

Reluctantly, Anna continued to read from the perfume-scented letter:

Richard must be in Boston for business and will have little need of my company. I know that after so many years it is bold of me to ask, but I so want to see you! I would love to see Yardley again, too. I will be arriving on June 6.

Please, darling, say that I may come! I have missed you more than you will ever know!

Until then,
Christine

Graham remained silent, her hands clenched into tight fists against the stone railing. From where she was sitting, Anna could see her tremble.

"Graham?" she questioned softly, frightened by her reaction.

"Today is the fifth of June, isn't it?" Graham asked at length, her voice barely a whisper. She kept her face averted, struggling to control her emotions.

"Yes."

Graham turned abruptly, her eyes bleak. She clenched the head of her walking stick so tightly that the fine tendons in her hand strained against the skin. With an effort she forced her voice to be calm.

"If you don't mind, I'd like to finish the rest of the correspondence another day."

She had clearly been dismissed, and Anna struggled not to call out to her as Graham left. Graham had made it clear that her concern was not wanted. Nevertheless, Anna could not put the disturbing letter, nor the mysterious Christine, from her mind.

Anna spent a restless night, her sleep broken by half-formed dreams of dark winds and raging surf, and in their midst, a single lonely figure, hauntingly alone. She awoke still tired, with a strange sense of foreboding. As much as she tried to put the infuriating Graham Yardley from her mind, she couldn't. She looked for her at the cliff's edge each morning when she woke; she waited for the time when Graham would push open the doors to her study, affording Anna a glimpse of her; she listened for her footsteps in the hall at night, unable to sleep until Graham retired. She could no more ignore the letter and its effect on Graham than she could ignore her own heartbeat. Whether Graham welcomed it or not, Anna could not seem to stop caring about her. She dressed hurriedly and went to find Helen.

"Good morning," Helen greeted her, her arms filled with supplies from the pantry.

"Who is Christine?" Anna demanded, too stressed for diplomacy.

Helen looked shocked, setting jars and cans down on the table with a thump. "Why, she's just someone Graham knew a long time ago."

"Well," Anna announced grimly, "she's coming here today."

"*What?* How do you know?" Helen cried in alarm. This could only mean more trouble for all of them, and goodness only knew what it was going to do to Graham. "Are you sure?"

"A letter came from her yesterday."

"I see," Helen frowned, speaking almost to herself. "Now I understand why Graham was so out of sorts last evening."

"Well, I don't," Anna seethed. "What is going on? And don't give me that 'old friend' routine. Graham looked like she'd seen a ghost yesterday when that letter came."

"Well," Helen began carefully, "they *are* old friends, and they haven't seen each other in years. I imagine Graham was just surprised."

"Helen," Anna said threateningly. She knew the difference between surprise and shock. "I know this is Graham's private affair, but I saw what that letter did to her. You know better than I what she's been through this week. How much more do you think she can take? Please, I just want to help."

Helen realized it wasn't fair not to explain at least as much as she could, although there were some things only Graham could disclose. She motioned for Anna to sit down beside her as she poured them both some coffee. Helen spoke softly, her memories taking her back to a time so different, and a Graham Yardley Anna would scarcely recognize.

"They met at music school, although Christine was quite a bit younger. For a number of years they were inseparable. Those were tumultuous years for Graham. She was at the peak of her career and consumed with it. The last few years on tour, Christine traveled with her. I think Christine resented Graham's music; it took so much of Graham's attention. And Christine was the kind of girl who was used to attention. She was always trying to drag Graham off to some party, but Graham never let anything, or anyone, come between her and her music. Believe me, they had some pretty big rows about that. Still Christine came closer to distracting Graham than anyone could. Graham was infatuated with her, in some way, and she tried very hard to balance her career and her friendship with Christine. Don't get me wrong, Christine could be very charming; and I think she cared for Graham, in her own way. Still, there were some pretty nasty scenes toward the end. They were together the night of the accident."

"What happened?" Anna asked, forcing her voice to be calm. Something in her rebelled at the thought of anyone having that kind of influence over Graham. Especially not a woman who was determined to see Graham that day.

Helen shook her head sadly. "No one knows for sure. Graham has never spoken of it to anyone. They were on their way home from a post-performance reception for Graham. It was rumored they had fought at the party. When they found the car—" Helen stopped for a second, gathering herself. That horrible night still seemed like yesterday.

"The car had rolled over several times into a ditch," Helen continued haltingly. "It took them a long time to get them out. Graham was unconscious, her body covering Christine's. Her leg was crushed and she had a severe head injury. Christine was badly bruised, but otherwise untouched. They kept Christine in the hospital for a few days, and as soon as she was released, she left the area. We were all so concerned about Graham, we didn't hear until later that Christine had married within the year—Richard Blair, an attorney who worked for David Norcross. Graham asked for her soon after she regained consciousness. When she learned that Christine was alive and married, she never mentioned her again." Helen stopped. "I'm sorry, that's truly all I know. Graham never talked about any of it, and I couldn't bring myself to remind her of it."

"Poor Graham," Anna whispered, shaken by the story. Whatever their relationship had been, Graham had obviously cared deeply for Christine. Was there no end to the losses she had suffered that tragic night?

"I don't know how she's going to be, seeing Christine again," Helen said worriedly.

Anna wondered just what power Christine still held over Graham, and exactly how she intended to use it.

Anna was on her knees in the rhododendrons when a sleek black Jaguar pulled up the drive. An attractive redhead slid from the car, the hem of her expensive dress pulling up to reveal shapely legs. The woman glanced about and spied Anna. She walked toward her, looking puzzled.

"Hello," she said, studying Anna curiously. "Where did you come from? Should I remember you?"

Anna stood, uncomfortable under the woman's appraising gaze. She wiped the dust from her hands as she said, "No, I've only been here a few months."

"Do you mean to say you *live* here?"

"Yes, I do," Anna replied stiffly. "I'm Anna Reid."

"Christine Hunt-Blair." After slight hesitation, the woman offered a soft and well-manicured hand.

Anna was acutely aware of the calluses on her own palm. She regarded the haughty woman before her, trying not to dislike her. After all, they had only just met. The visitor surveyed her critically, then shrugged in dismissal, casting a disdainful eye toward the house.

"Yardley looks rather run down. I suppose it could use a caretaker. Poor old Helen probably can't cope any longer, and Graham wouldn't notice if the house were falling down around her, as long as it didn't fall on the piano." After a moment's pause, she added, "From what I understand, of course, Graham has no reason to care what it looks like any more."

Anna was stunned by the heartless remark. It was inconceivable to her that anyone could make light of Graham's injury, especially the woman who had supposedly been so close to Graham. What on earth had Graham found attractive in this shallow, insensitive woman? *Maybe it's the fact that she's exceptionally beautiful*, Anna couldn't help thinking, flushed with a possessive anger that only confused her more.

Oblivious to Anna's indignation, Christine announced, "I've come to see Graham. Where is she?"

"I imagine she's in the music room," Anna replied stiffly. "She usually is this time of day. If you'll give me a moment, I'll take you in."

"Oh, there's no need," Christine laughed, turning toward the house. "I should have known that's where she'd be. I know my way quite well."

Anna watched her retreating back, feeling more than a little foolish. After all, this had nothing to do with her. Her mood did not lighten when she entered the kitchen an hour later to find Helen preparing an elaborate dinner.

"Graham asked that we have dinner in the dining room tonight. I was so surprised; we haven't had a formal meal in there for years. And I've barely had time to prepare." She was clearly harried, hurrying to arrange appetizers on a large silver platter while she watched over other items in the oven and on the stove.

"Can I help?" Anna asked dutifully. *My, Christine certainly is getting the red carpet treatment*, she thought resentfully. She was immediately embarrassed by her response. *What in God's name is the matter with me?*

"Oh no dear. This is the most excitement I've had in years." Helen laughed. "Of course, in previous years, if Graham were entertaining, I always had help in the kitchen, and a butler to serve. Thank goodness there are only a few of us tonight."

"I don't think I'll be joining you," Anna said. She didn't think she'd enjoy watching Graham and Christine reminisce, and she didn't think she could tolerate Christine's proprietary attitude.

Helen stopped what she was doing, taking conscious notice of Anna for the first time. She had that tight look around her mouth she got when she was upset, and it didn't take much to think what that might be about.

"Have you met Christine?" Helen questioned cautiously.

Anna was usually calm and good-natured, but she had a temper where things concerned Graham.

"Briefly, in the drive. Is she with Graham?" Anna couldn't help but ask, as much as she had promised herself she wouldn't think about them.

"She's waiting for Graham in the library as Graham instructed," Helen informed her. "Graham specifically asked me to inform you of dinner, my dear. I'm sure she expects you to be there."

"And I don't suppose she would broker any debate," Anna sighed in resignation. *Oh well, I can stand it for one meal*, she thought as she left for her room.

Anna never would have lingered by the open door if she hadn't caught a glimpse of Graham entering the library. Anna stopped in surprise when she saw her. Graham had obviously dressed with care for her meeting with Christine. She was resplendent in a starched, finely pleated white tuxedo shirt and formal black-striped trousers. A blood red cummerbund encircled her narrow waist; gold and diamond cuff links sparkled on the stiff French cuffs of her sleeves. Her barber must have come, because her usually unruly mane was trimmed and expertly styled. She looked ready for the concert stage. Anna stared, knowing she had never seen anyone so magnificent. If she hadn't been so taken by that tantalizing view of the woman she had hitherto only imagined from photographs, she never would have witnessed the scene that would come to haunt her unmercifully.

"Graham, darling!" Christine cried as Graham stepped into the room. She rushed to her, one arm outstretched, catching Graham's right hand in hers. "Oh, my darling, you look even more exquisite than I remembered," she said throatily.

Graham lifted Christine's hand, bowing her head to brush her lips across the soft skin.

"Hello, Christine," she murmured.

Christine slid her other hand into Graham's hair, raising Graham's head. "Is that any way to greet me after all this time?" she questioned breathlessly. Not waiting for a reply, she stepped forward and pressed her lips to Graham's.

Anna turned from the door as Graham pulled Christine firmly into her embrace.

Anna stood staring out her bedroom window, seeing nothing of the view. She kept searching for something to erase the image of Christine in Graham's arms. She kept searching for some way to lessen the terrible desolation the vision produced. She kept asking herself why she felt this way, and she kept running from the answer.

She finally forced herself to perform some normal task. She was after all expected at dinner. She showered and was just pulling on one of her fancier blouses when a knock on her door interrupted her. She finished buttoning hastily as she crossed the room. Pulling open the door, she was astonished to find Graham standing in the hall. Graham had donned a midnight blue silk dinner jacket, and she was more than stunning. Anna tried desperately to quell the surge of jealousy, knowing that Christine had prompted this display. *Why should I be jealous? I must be losing my mind.*

"Anna?" Graham questioned, surprised by the silence.

"Yes?" Anna responded, more abruptly than she had intended. All she wanted in that moment was to get away from Graham Yardley and the unsettling emotions she provoked. "What is it? Do you need something?"

Graham smiled slightly and shook her head. "May I speak with you a moment?"

"Of course," Anna replied, becoming alarmed. Graham had never come to her room before. She stepped aside to allow Graham entry. "Sit down, please. The chairs are before the fireplace, where they've always been."

Anna found Graham's expression impossible to decipher. She waited while Graham made her way without faltering to the seating area. She followed somewhat reluctantly, sitting anxiously in the opposite chair.

"I wanted to tell you myself that Christine will be staying here at Yardley for some indefinite time," Graham began in a low voice. "Apparently, she is thinking of leaving her husband and needs time to consider her future."

Anna's heart lurched, and for once she was glad that Graham couldn't see her face. Christine to stay at Yardley. As if it weren't perfectly clear what Christine expected her future to be. You only had to look at the way she looked at Graham to know her intentions. Anna was too upset to notice that Graham did not appear overly happy with her announcement.

"Does this mean that you won't need my services any longer?" Anna asked, trying unsuccessfully to keep her voice from shaking. Her mind recoiled from the thought of leaving Yardley. This was her life.

Graham sat forward in alarm. "Good God, no! Why ever would you think that? You belong here at Yardley, and I would want you to stay as long as you are happy here. I merely wanted to tell you about Christine myself, so that you wouldn't be surprised at dinner." She couldn't believe that Anna would imagine she wanted her to leave. That thought was the farthest thing from her mind. In fact, it was unthinkable. "Anna, please don't be upset. It wasn't my intention to concern you. This has been a difficult day for me. I'm sorry."

For the first time, Anna noticed the tremor in Graham's hands. Her resolve to distance herself from Graham disappeared as soon as she recognized her distress. She was helpless in the face of Graham's need. She simply couldn't bear to see her like this. Grasping her hand, she said softly, "It's all right. Please don't worry about me."

Graham bowed her head, gripping Anna's fingers tightly for a moment before abruptly rising. She began to pace, agitated. "I couldn't turn her away, Anna. Not after—after all we'd been to each other." She sighed, knowing her words were inadequate. How could she begin to explain what she could barely grasp herself? When she heard Christine's letter the day before, she had been plunged instantly back into that dark night, into the twisted wreckage of her car. Her last memory was of Christine trying to escape from her. She had imagined Christine's return so many times, dreamed of Christine telling her it was all a nightmare, that she had come home. Month after torturous month she had waited in the silent darkness of her rooms, listening for the quick footfalls in the hall that signaled Christine's arrival. More than a year had passed before she would believe that Christine was truly gone. The day she accepted that was the day she accepted her blindness, and the knowledge that the music had abandoned her as well. In an instant her life was devoid of everything that had given it meaning. She had neither the hope nor the desire to fill the emptiness with anything, or anyone, else. And so she had accepted her fate without protest, allowing time to pass unnoticed. These last few months since Anna's arrival were her only clear moments in the long torturous years since her world had shattered. Only the fragrance of the flowers, and the memory of Anna's hand on her arm as they strolled through the gardens, brought a faint smile to her lips.

The thought of confronting Christine brought only confusion, instead of the celebration she imagined she should experience. She spent the previous night awake, leaving the chair where she passed the evening hours to walk through the gardens before dawn. When she felt the first warmth of the sun's rays on her skin, she returned to the house for her preparations.

It was important to her that Christine see her as she had once been, not as the shell of a being she had become. Pity from anyone was intolerable, but it would be devastating from the one woman who had claimed to have loved her. It seemed from Christine's greeting that she had succeeded in that at least. Christine's kiss still lingered on her lips, and the words that followed were still fresh in her mind.

"I've missed that so much," Christine whispered against her neck. "You were the only one who ever made me feel so alive."

It had seemed the most natural thing in the world to take Christine into her arms, to bend her head to the lips she knew so well, to hear the soft intake of breath she remembered with startling clarity. Christine stirred against her as she had a thousand times before, softly moaning her name. Nothing had changed, and everything was different.

Graham saw them together in her mind's eye, but her body remained untouched. Whereas once the mere stroke of Christine's fingers against her skin could make her heart race, now she felt no surging of her blood, no flaring of her senses, no answering passion. Gently, she loosed her hold on the woman in her arms, stepping back from her embrace.

Christine had always been able to read Graham's mercurial moods. "You don't believe I've missed you, do you, darling?"

"Perhaps if it had been a year, or two, or even ten," Graham replied without anger, for strangely she felt none, "I might have."

Christine slowly traced the faint scar across Graham's forehead, then reached up to kiss her lips once more. "Give me time. I'll make you believe again," she whispered.

Graham shook her head, in disbelief then, in wordless frustration now. She knew Anna was waiting. "I'm sorry, Anna. I wish I could explain. There's simply nothing I can say."

"That's all right," Anna said stiffly. "You don't need to say anything. She is clearly important to you, and it certainly isn't necessary to justify yourself to me." She knew she sounded cold, but she couldn't help it. She wasn't even certain what bothered her so much about Christine's return. If Christine could ease Graham's deep desolation, if she could restore some happiness to Graham's life, Anna should be grateful. Of course, Anna wanted to see Graham happy. Oh, it was all too much to deal with, this whole nightmare of a week. Why was it that the very things that seemed to ease Graham's discomfort—her physical reserve, her emotional distance, and now Christine's presence—were the same things that made Anna so miserable?

"I'll be down for dinner, Graham," Anna said wearily.

Graham started to speak, then merely sighed. "Yes."

CHAPTER ELEVEN

A nna was the first to arrive in the dining room. The long highly polished table was elaborately set with starched handmade linens, antique silver cutlery, fine crystal glassware and china place settings. The formality of the scene was more than a little daunting. Anna reminded herself that there had been much more to Graham's previous life than she had gleaned from the newspaper accounts. The understated way Graham lived at Yardley now must be a far departure from her earlier life. She was a world-renowned artist, recognized in every civilized country, and surely she would have traveled in the most elite circles. She would have been feted at every turn. It made Anna wistful to think she would never know that part of Graham.

Angrily she reminded herself that Graham Yardley obviously had all the companionship she needed with the arrival of Christine. Whatever diversion Anna had provided was surely unnecessary now. The only person who would miss their moments together was herself. She felt at once helpless and irrationally saddened.

"My don't you look nice," Helen exclaimed as she bustled into the room, mercifully delivering Anna from her introspection.

"Helen," Anna greeted her with relief. "You must have been working for hours in here. It's wonderful."

Helen beamed with pleasure as she began setting up the large buffet along one side of the room. "You're right, I did. And it couldn't have been a happier chore. For just a moment there this morning, when she was telling me what she wanted done, Graham seemed like her old self."

Helen had no idea that her words had wounded Anna, who instantly thought that all it had taken to motivate Graham's recovery was Christine's return.

Helen continued, unaware of Anna's growing depression. "I do wish she would let me serve, though. She insisted that I prepare a buffet, and that I eat with you, but it just doesn't seem right. If only I had time I could have found help."

"I don't have much experience, but I could probably manage the serving," Anna said dubiously. In her state of mind, anything seemed preferable to sitting down to dinner with Graham and Christine.

"Nonsense," Graham said from the door, having heard Anna's remark. "I'm sure we can all manage ourselves just this once, Helen."

Anna turned at the sound of Graham's voice, her heart freezing at the sight of Graham and Christine together. Christine, who had changed into a revealing black evening dress, stood with her arm wrapped through Graham's, leaning slightly so that her body pressed against Graham's side. They made a stunningly attractive couple, and Anna had to admit that's exactly what they were. There was a connection between them that was undeniable, regardless of the years that had separated them. Christine held onto Graham as if she owned her, and Graham seemed content to let her. Anna averted her gaze, unable to tolerate the insurmountable evidence that Graham was still very much involved with Christine.

"At least let me help you set up," she said to Helen, grateful for any diversion.

"Thank you, dear," Helen replied kindly. Anna's reaction to Graham's entrance had not escaped her. She could only imagine what the poor girl was thinking. And she probably didn't know Graham well enough to realize that Graham was behaving exactly as she would with any guest at Yardley.

"You really didn't need to open the guest room for me, Helen," Christine commented as she allowed Graham to seat her to Graham's right at the table. She smiled without the slightest trace of warmth, her gaze fixed on Anna. "It wasn't necessary, you know."

Anna glanced at Graham, whose face remained expressionless. But Christine had made her point, if she wanted to make it clear where she intended to sleep. Why Christine felt it necessary that she understand her claim on Graham, Anna couldn't imagine. As if it would make a difference even if she *did* care. She gritted her teeth and resolved to make this the last meal she shared with Graham Yardley and her Christine.

The dinner proved to be every bit as difficult to endure as Anna feared. Graham, although attentive to Christine's needs and unfailingly courteous, remained distant and distracted throughout the meal.

Christine appeared not to notice Graham's preoccupation, regaling them with social gossip and endless anecdotes of her travels. It did not escape Anna's notice that Christine never once mentioned anything remotely to do with music. For her part, Anna had nothing to contribute, and remained silent. She breathed a sigh of relief when at last she could depart with the excuse of helping Helen clear the table.

"You know you don't have to do this, dear," Helen chided when Anna joined her in the kitchen. "But I do appreciate it."

"I work here, too," Anna said, more sharply than she intended. "Believe me, it's a pleasure compared to sitting in there."

Helen studied her speculatively. "I gather the company wasn't to your liking," she commented mildly.

"It was wonderful to finally share a meal with Graham," Anna admitted. She had enjoyed Graham's presence immensely, despite Graham's obvious distraction. Anna only wished it hadn't required Christine's arrival to prompt Graham to join them.

"Christine can be a bit overbearing, but you must remember she's always been indulged by everyone."

"Including Graham apparently," Anna said ungraciously. She sighed in disgust, as much with herself as the situation. "Oh, I don't know, Helen, it just annoys me the way she hovers over Graham. She poured her wine; she served her food—the next thing you know she'll be cutting her meat. You know very well Graham doesn't need that kind of help."

"Maybe that's the only kind of help Christine has to offer," Helen suggested sagely.

Anna stopped what she was doing and stared at Helen. "What are you saying, Helen?"

"Christine has always been more glitter than substance. And Graham has always demanded a great deal from people. Even before their accident, Christine was frightened by Graham's intensity. If she were to truly confront Graham's needs now, she would be overwhelmed."

Well, she certainly seems to be meeting some of Graham's needs without any problems, Anna thought angrily. She knew she couldn't discuss Christine rationally, not with the scene in the library so fresh in her memory. Every time she thought of her, she saw Graham bending to kiss her.

"I don't know what I'm saying any longer," Anna said wearily. "I think I just need to get some rest. I'm going to say goodnight to Graham and head upstairs."

She found Graham and Christine just rising from the table upon her return. Before she could say her goodnights, Christine spoke, seemingly oblivious to Anna's presence.

"Why don't you play something for me, darling?" she asked, grasping Graham's hand.

Graham could have been carved from marble, she was so still. Slowly, she disengaged Christine's fingers from hers, moving Christine's hand to the crook of her arm. When she spoke, her voice was carefully neutral. "I think not. I need to work."

"Surely you're not going to work tonight?" Christine protested, her cheeks flushed with ire.

"Yes," Graham replied with finality.

For an instant Anna thought Christine was about to argue, but the other woman wisely relented. Nevertheless, her voice was cold.

"All right, if you must. But do promise me you'll breakfast with me."

Graham nodded. "Of course. Now let me show you to your room."

As she led Christine from the room, she said softly, "Goodnight, Anna."

For Anna it was anything but a good night. She tried to read, but she couldn't concentrate. She dozed off in her chair, only to be awakened by a noise in the hall. She knew Graham's step by now. The person passing by her door toward the master suite was not Graham Yardley.

There was no doubt, of course, about what she had witnessed earlier in the library. It was clear from what Helen had said and from what she herself had witnessed that Graham and Christine had been lovers before their accident. It seemed apparent that they were about to resume that relationship now. Graham obviously had never stopped loving Christine—that was the real reason she had secluded herself for so many long and lonely years. Anna wasn't disturbed by the physical nature of their relationship, but she was stunned by her own response to that kiss. She couldn't bear to think of Graham making love to Christine. That reaction was something she had no reference for, and she was at a loss as to how to cope. She told herself she should be pleased that

Graham had a chance at happiness, but what she felt instead was a deep sense of loss. Anna's emotions were in turmoil. One thing she knew for certain—she could not face them together in the morning.

After a fitful few hours of tossing and turning, she rose just before dawn, dressed by the last of the moonlight, and went out for a walk. Unconsciously she followed the path Graham took each morning down the steep slope to the edge of the cliff. She stood where she had seen Graham stand. Anna closed her eyes and tried to imagine what it was that drew Graham to this lonely precipice. After a moment, she thought she knew. Waves crashed below with a deafening roar, sending needles of spray hundreds of feet up the cliff. The air was so sharp it stung her skin. The wind blew harder here, fresh from over the water, carrying the rich scent of sea life. It was much colder on the exposed bluff as well. This would be the first place at Yardley where the morning sun would fall. Condensed in this one spot, in the dark just before dawn, the senses were so assaulted, you did not need to see to know the essence of the world around you. For a brief instant each day, on the edge of this cliff, Graham Yardley was not blind.

Anna leaned against the stone wall that rimmed the cliff and cried. She cried for Graham, for all she had been, and all she had lost. She cried for herself, because she loved her, and would never know her. She cried for the years she had spent not knowing herself, only to discover too late what form her love truly took. As she cried, the harsh wind dried her tears. When the first faint wisps of summer sunlight flickered across her cheeks, she opened her eyes to a day that dawned clearer, and lonelier, than any she had ever known. She sat on a worn weathered bench to watch the sunrise, and that's where Graham found her.

"Anna?" came the deep voice she could never mistake for another's.

Anna looked up to find Graham beside her, in the same clothes she had worn to dinner, rumpled and exhausted.

"How do you always know?" she asked quietly.

Graham smiled faintly. "The air moves differently when you're near."

"You should have been a poet, not a pianist," Anna breathed around the tears that threatened again. "Although maybe there isn't any difference. Please, sit down."

Graham acquiesced, stretching her long legs out before her, leaning back with a sigh. Her hand lightly grazed Anna's shoulder where she rested it along the top of the bench.

"How is your work coming?" Anna asked, unsettled by Graham's nearness, but loathe to move away.

Graham shrugged tiredly. "I wish I knew. I'm trying only to capture the essence of what I'm hearing. I don't dare analyze it yet. I'm afraid to discover it is trash."

"Have you slept?"

"Ah, Anna—always so concerned. Why do you care?" she asked not unkindly. Anna's caring confounded her. Many people in her life had professed to care about her, but only Helen remained, and she had loved Graham all her life. Why a stranger should extend kindness now, when she was bereft of all her talents, she could not comprehend.

"Because I—" Anna hesitated over words she was not prepared to face. "Because you deserve to be cared about Graham. And you're avoiding my question. Did you sleep?"

"As much as one can in one of those godforsaken chairs from the last century," Graham admitted. "Anna," she continued with a weary sigh, "tell me about something you love. Tell me about something beyond my view."

As Anna spoke, Graham's tension ebbed, and her breathing grew quiet and deep. Anna told of her favorite cities, the movies that made her cry, and the books she had read a dozen times. She talked of her family, and her friends, and her dreams. She talked long after she thought Graham was asleep, because she wanted to keep her near, because it pleased her to imagine that some part of Graham heard her secrets. When at last she fell silent, the day was fully born.

"So," Graham murmured, to Anna's surprise awake after all. "You love New York City, French movies with subtitles, wild flowers, and—what else?"

I love you, she answered from her soul. "Yardley," Anna whispered with an ache in her heart, "I love Yardley."

"Yes," Graham uttered as she pushed herself upright. "I can tell that you do." She frowned as she turned her gaze toward the old house. "Is it seven-thirty yet?"

"Seven-twenty," Anna confirmed.

"I must say good-bye then. I have a breakfast engagement."

Anna spoke without thinking. "Surely Christine will understand if you get some sleep. You've been up all night."

"I'm afraid that Christine never had any patience when my work disrupted her plans," Graham remarked calmly. "I'm sure that's one thing that hasn't changed."

She leaned to brush her hand along Anna's shoulder. "Thank you for these moments of peace, Anna. I'll see you at dinner."

With that she was gone, and Anna was left with an empty day looming ahead.

When Anna returned from running errands, grateful for any mindless task to divert her thoughts from Graham, she was unreasonably glad to see that Christine's Jaguar was no longer parked in the drive, even if only temporarily. Just the sight of it was unsettling. Instead, the familiar truck bearing the logo *Womenworks* was parked in its place. Daphne Herrald and her two woman crew were the landscapers she had hired for the heavy clearing and hauling that needed to be done. She not only liked their work, she liked the women. They were working full-time at Yardley now, and Anna planned on keeping them on part-time after the summer. They were fast, efficient and friendly. And most importantly, they seemed to appreciate Graham's special circumstances. It was impossible to tell when Graham might take it upon herself to stroll down one of the many garden paths, or decide that she wanted something from the kitchen garden. After Graham's mishaps with her own carelessness, and the near disaster with the painter, Anna was always worried. Without Anna watching over them, these women were meticulous with their tools and careful to clean up after themselves.

Anna noticed Graham and Daphne deep in conversation as she rounded the corner from the drive. Graham, leaning one hip against the balustrade in her familiar stance, hands in pockets, smiled down at Daphne who stood several steps below her on the walk. Daphne looked tanned, fit, and if the expression on her face was any indication, quite taken with the master of Yardley Manor. Daphne and the women on her crew made it no secret that they were lesbians, and it certainly hadn't mattered one way or the other to Anna—until now. If Daphne wasn't looking at Graham with something very close to lust in her eyes, Anna was sadly mistaken.

The low-pitched murmur of Graham's sonorous voice reached her, and as always, Anna was stirred by it. Seeing Graham and Daphne together, as innocent as it surely was, made Anna realize how much Graham's physical presence affected her. She had thought her strikingly handsome from the first night they met. She found herself captivated by the delicacy and sinewy strength of Graham's hands as she sketched a phrase in the air. The wind blowing Graham's hair into disarray always left her wanting to brush the locks off her forehead. And she could scarcely look into her fathomless dark eyes without feeling something twist deep within her.

She nearly gasped as all the images which were Graham cascaded through her and left her unmistakably wanting her. In that instant, she understood fully her aversion to Christine. It was knowing that Graham had once loved her—perhaps did still—and the fact that Graham touched her with love. Anger raged within her when she thought of Graham wasting her precious passion on someone who did not cherish it—on someone who had abandoned her when Graham's need was greatest. Anna understood with sudden startling clarity exactly what she wanted. She wanted Graham's passion, in all its forms, for herself. The insight was so undeniable that it left her staggered. She couldn't question her desire; her body ached with it.

She turned away from the women in the garden. Her reaction to the sight of Daphne and Graham together followed too closely on the heels of Christine's arrival. She seemed to be assaulted at every turn with her longing for Graham, and the impossibility of her desire. Foolishly, she had allowed herself to believe that Graham felt something of the connection she herself could not deny each time she saw her, or heard her step in the hall, or her music in the air. She should have known that for a woman of Graham's intensity and unrelenting passion, her love for Christine would be inextinguishable.

Anna fled into the house, desperately trying to escape her own heart. She stood unpacking groceries, her mind strangely blank when a short rap on the door interrupted her.

"Hey." Daphne said as she pushed open the door. "I thought I saw you drive up. Can I talk to you a sec?"

Anna nodded distractedly. "Sure."

"You're getting a lot of soil erosion on the edges of the paths, especially on the back slopes. What do you think about putting in some ground cover along there? It's labor intensive to do the planting, but in the end it will preserve the area," Daphne stated. She looked at Anna curiously when she didn't answer.

"Anna? You okay?"

Anna forced herself to focus. "Yes, sure—ground cover? I had noticed that, but there's so much around here that needs attention, it just slipped my mind. Did you speak to Graham about it?"

Daphne looked surprised. "No, why would I? You hired me. You make the decisions."

"I just thought—I saw you talking to Graham when I came home—" Her voice trailed off uncertainly. *God, I'm a mess.*

"Oh, that was just small talk. I ran into her out back, she asked me how things were going. She's always so *charming*, you know? Every woman in my crew has a crush on her," she said with a laugh.

"Including you?" Anna asked, trying to match Daphne's light tone.

Daphne studied Anna carefully. She looked shaken and pale.

"Oh hell—is that what you're thinking? I have a lover I'm nuts about, and we've got two great kids. Graham is fascinating, not to mention gorgeous, and I *do* think she's incredibly attractive, but looking is as far as it goes with me."

Anna busied herself with unpacking, avoiding Daphne's intense gaze. "It's none of my business anyway. I didn't mean to put you on the spot."

"I assumed you two were lovers," Daphne said, a question in her voice.

"No," Anna whispered almost to herself. Taking a deep breath, she turned to Daphne. "Why did you think that?"

"I could be on dangerous ground here—lots of room to offend if I'm wrong." Daphne shrugged, flashing her trademark grin. "But what the hell. After twenty years of seeing women in all stages of togetherness, you get a sense for it. It's the way you *are* around each other. Your face lights up whenever she appears. Your eyes follow her whenever she's in sight. I know damn well it kills you every time she heads down that goddamned slope to the cliff. I can tell you stop breathing. It takes more guts than I've got to watch her do that without screaming."

"Graham doesn't leave you any choice," Anna murmured, "She doesn't know how to be anything but proud."

Daphne nodded. "I've never met anyone like her. She listens for you, you know. In the middle of our conversation just now I saw her smile, and her whole body relaxed just a little. Ten seconds later I heard your Jeep. She'd been listening for you to come home. She knows how to find you when you're in the garden. She walks right to you. How does she *do* that?"

"I don't know," Anna sighed. "I don't think I know anything about anything anymore."

Daphne considered letting it go, but Anna looked so miserable. Graham had seemed pretty frayed too. "First time you've ever been in love with a woman?" she asked kindly.

Hearing it put so matter-of-factly gave her pause. "I've never been in love before," she said after a moment, knowing it was true.

"Sometimes," Daphne continued cautiously, "it's just a false alarm."

Anna met Daphne's gaze steadily, a muscle tightening in her jaw. "No."

Daphne could tell she meant it. And something was really wrong. Anna's usually clear blue eyes were clouded with pain, her face was drawn and tired, and she looked on the verge of breaking into tears. "Does she know how you feel about her?"

Anna studied her hands, her cheeks coloring. "It's not that simple. Graham is—complicated. She was horribly hurt." She took a deep breath, smiling tremulously. "I don't think Graham gives me much thought."

"This is serious, isn't it?" Daphne asked softly.

"Yes."

"I wish I could help—" Daphne began.

Anna appreciated her sympathy, but she interrupted her with a shake of her head. Even before Christine's arrival, Anna noticed a reticence in the way Graham treated her. She was always welcoming and seemed to enjoy Anna's company, but still there was the distance. Just when Anna thought Graham was becoming more comfortable with her, something would cause her to withdraw. Anna was never sure what she had said, or what painful memory she had triggered. Often Anna's encounters with Graham left her unsettled, and she was slowly becoming aware of an inner void that seemed to deepen each day. With Christine here now, and Graham's apparent attachment to her, there seemed to be little room for Anna in Graham's life. She smiled at Daphne ruefully.

"The only one who can help is Graham."

CHAPTER TWELVE

In the days that followed, Anna saw little of Graham. She kept to her usual routine, spending time with Helen in the morning, working on the grounds in the afternoon. Graham had not sent for her, and Anna did not seek her out. She often saw Graham and Christine together as they walked about the grounds, or sat together on the terrace in the afternoons. Graham spent every evening, if not the entire night, alone in her study.

Aside from the times Graham denied her entry to the music room, Christine was never far from Graham's side, and her possessive attitude was intolerable for Anna. Anna tried her best to be polite, but the sight of them together, Christine constantly touching Graham in some way, made her irrationally angry. And that made her even more short-tempered. After all, it was none of her concern if Graham Yardley behaved like a fool around that woman. She began to wonder how much more she could endure. She tried to avoid them as much as possible, even taking her meals with Helen in the late afternoon, offering excuses as to why she couldn't be present for the now routine dinner gatherings. The worst parts of her day were the evenings. Although she usually worked until she was physically exhausted, she didn't seem able to sleep. Once it had been a comfort to retire to her rooms, and fall asleep with a book open on her lap. Now even that consolation eluded her. Every time someone passed in the hall she couldn't help thinking it was Christine, on her way to the master suite at the opposite end of the hall. Rationally, she knew there was any number of reasons Helen or Christine or Graham herself might pass in the hall, but she was anything but rational. She was driving herself crazy imagining Christine in Graham's bed.

She threw down the book she had been trying to read for three nights in a row and snatched her denim jacket from the coat rack by her door. Despite the warm early summer days, evenings by the sea were still cool. She needed to walk off her anxiety and deepening sense of despair. Unconsciously, she took the meandering path through the lower slopes of the back property, skirting along the sea wall. Yardley stood several hundred yards uphill, and with its lights flickering through the trees, it cast a magical shape against the darkening sky. As if to accompany that otherworldly aura, Anna caught the strains of a wistful melody floating in the air. She began the steep climb up the wildly overgrown track toward the source. The terrace doors stood open, the blackness within the music room embracing the darkness of the night. Graham was alone, playing.

Anna leaned against the balustrade on the far side of the terrace, listening, straining for some glimpse of the woman in the shadows. The melancholy tenor of the music seemed to echo her own internal anguish. She made no effort to stop the tears. She had no idea how long she stood there, joined with Graham in some unnamed longing, when a voice quite near startled her from her reverie.

"She is absolutely magnificent, isn't she?" Christine remarked casually as she joined Anna on the terrace.

"Yes," Anna said softly, having no reason to deny what the entire world had recognized. Only a few of her caliber born each century, one reviewer had said.

"Oh, I wasn't talking about her music," Christine laughed. "But then I'm sure you've noticed what an exquisite specimen she is. You seem to have developed quite an appreciation for all her attributes. Believe me, in her case, her genius extends beyond the piano. She brings that remarkable intensity to absolutely *everything* she touches. And everyone. Fortunately Graham was too seduced by her music to notice anyone for more than a night or two—before me of course."

She laughed, appraising Anna in the dim light of the moon. She found Anna naturally lovely, with her work- hardened body, feminine yet strong, and her clear eyes and shimmering hair. She was the type Christine had amused herself with over the years since Graham. *Under other circumstances*, she thought briefly, then reminded herself of her intentions.

"Now you did surprise me at first," she continued mockingly. "I wouldn't have thought you'd find Graham to your tastes, although God knows women of all persuasions used to throw themselves at her. And *living* here with her—I can imagine that would be a temptation even if women weren't your usual pleasure."

"I was just on my way in," Anna said as she made to leave. She had no intention of allowing Christine to goad her into a discussion of her feelings for Graham. And she was in real danger of doing her bodily harm if she stayed.

"You're no match for the competition, you know," Christine said lightly.

Anna stopped abruptly, incensed. "I am not competing with you," she seethed.

Christine laughed, tossing her head in dismissal. "Perhaps not, although from the way you look at her, I think you're deluding yourself. Unfortunately, Graham has no way of knowing what's in your eyes, does she?"

She pushed away from the balcony railing, stepping quite close to Anna as she did so. Anna could smell her fragrant perfume.

"I wasn't speaking of myself, although knowing Graham, I have no concerns. I'd wager she's much too honorable to take you to her bed just for sport. Although I'm sure you wouldn't take much convincing, would you?" She ran a finger lightly down Anna's arm, laughing again when Anna hastily pulled away. "She is too hopelessly romantic to let old passions fade, and unlike you, I'm not above physical persuasion. Regardless of what she says, her body never lies."

She touched Anna's hand ever so lightly as she passed into the night. "I was speaking of the music, my dear innocent. The music is Graham's true mistress."

With that she was gone, leaving Anna to stare after her with a mixture of anger and pity. She had issued some kind of warning, although Anna couldn't imagine why she felt it necessary. God only knew, Anna was no threat to her claim on Graham's affections. What amazed her was that a woman who had supposedly loved Graham Yardley for over two decades did not understand what Anna realized the moment she heard Graham play. Music was not Graham's mistress; music was Graham's life. To love Graham was to welcome the force that sustained her, even though it threatened to destroy her as she struggled to bring it forth from her soul. Anna could no more be jealous of Graham's music than she could be jealous of her indomitable will, or her passionate ardor, or her sensitive spirit. The day the music truly deserted her would be the day her heart ceased to beat. Anna prayed for the day the music would flow unbidden from Graham's soul, for then she would be truly healed.

Anna glanced once more into the darkened room, imagining Graham absorbed in the sound, comforted by her nearness.

Graham's music lingered in Anna's mind throughout the morning as she occupied herself with outside work. She spent most of the time with contractors and subcontractors and by noon she was ready for a break. She wandered down to the stone bench under the huge sycamore, recalling wistfully the afternoon she and Graham had spent there. She turned from the memory of the brief closeness they had shared. It only made their estrangement harder. She stretched out on the bench in the dappled shade afforded by the overhanging branches, draped one arm over her eyes, and slept. When she slowly approached consciousness again, she was aware she was not alone. Even without opening her eyes, she sensed her.

"How long have you been here?" Anna questioned, rolling onto her side to study the woman seated on the ground, her back against the bench where Anna lay. She looked weary in a way that went beyond fatigue, but the strain belied by a tightness in her fine jaw was absent. She seemed strangely peaceful.

Graham turned her head toward Anna's voice with a soft smile, a smile that eased the tension from her face. Anna's heart turned over at the sight of her vulnerable beauty. "Not long—an hour, I think," Graham replied.

"What have you been doing?" Anna asked tenderly, brushing a stray twig from Graham's dark hair.

Graham shuddered involuntarily at the light touch that strayed unintentionally against her cheek. As often as Christine touched her, nothing she did affected her like this. Graham felt the first tingle of caution even as she warmed to the touch. She must take care where Anna was concerned, yet she couldn't seem to do without her company. These last few weeks since Christine's arrival had been doubly hard. She had to contend with Christine's constant demands for her attention, and her persistent attempts to rekindle Graham's ardor. Along with that, Graham had little time to spend with Anna. She missed her humor, and her compassion, and her wonderful way of bringing life to Graham's inner vision. Just her quiet, soothing tone brought Graham some semblance of calm. Graham found she even missed Anna's dauntless insistence that she sleep, or eat, or get out of the sun—the kind of demand Graham had never accepted of anyone. She had been lonely for a kind of connection she no longer thought she needed. She tried to ignore the growing agitation and discomfort for days, but finally, almost against her will, she had gone in search of her young employee. Finding her asleep, she had been content just to be near her.

"I was listening to you breathe, thinking that the cadence was much like a refrain. Suddenly the music I've been trying to compose began pouring through my mind," Graham said slowly, as if speaking in a dream. She was amazed at how easily it had come, after all the solitary struggle night after night to no avail, just by sitting quietly with a sleeping woman. "I've just been here listening," she finished quietly.

Anna watched the transformation of Graham's face as she spoke. The tense muscles softened, the fine lines about her eyes and lips relaxed, and suddenly she looked years younger. When Graham sighed and leaned her head back, it took all of Anna's control not to guide Graham's head into her lap. She wanted to hold her desperately. Only her fear that Graham would retreat, as she had so often, stilled her hand.

"I'm so happy for you," Anna said quietly.

Graham reached for Anna's hand, taking her by surprise. "I believe that you are." She brushed her lips softly across Anna's hand, then laid it gently down. With a sigh, she pushed herself upright. There were issues she needed to attend to, no matter how pleasant her moments here had been.

"I have consented to Christine's desire to give a small dinner party in honor of Helen's birthday. I would like you to attend," Graham stated flatly.

"Oh, Graham, I don't think so. I don't really belong there," Anna said in a rush. She couldn't imagine a worse scenario. Trapped with Christine at some formal affair.

Graham shook her head slightly. "You *do* belong. Helen cares for you a great deal, and you are a part of this household. I want you there."

Still Anna protested. "I *work* for you, Graham. I'm not part of your social world."

"I have no social world, Anna," Graham remarked darkly, all semblance of her recent serenity gone. "There will be some family friends, people Helen has known for years, and some recent acquaintances of Christine. If it weren't for the fact that Helen has had precious little thanks for the task of looking after Yardley all this time, I wouldn't hear of it." She ran a hand through her hair, glowering at some distant vision, before she continued wearily, "It will be difficult enough for me—I need you there."

Anna could not fathom the reason, but there was little she could do in the face of Graham's direct plea. "Of course, I'll be there."

Graham nodded. "Good." Looking as if she were about to leave, she turned abruptly and cast Anna a serious look. "And I'll expect you at dinner from now on, Anna. Every night."

Not waiting for a reply, she stepped out from the shadow of the tree, disappearing into the bright sunlight, leaving Anna staring after her.

CHAPTER THIRTEEN

G uests had gathered in the foyer of the ballroom, which had been opened and refurbished under Anna's watchful direction the entire previous week. Helen, as the honoree, was seated on a plush velvet sofa, conversing with friends and sampling the ample hor d'ouerves and endless champagne. Tuxedo-clad young women moved through the crowd offering food and drink. Anna kept one eye on the kitchen, making sure the caterers had every thing they needed, and the other on the grand staircase that flanked the reception area. Even though it was nearly the appointed time for dinner to be served, neither Graham nor Christine had arrived. She was about to signal the maitre d' to begin seating people when a low murmur of excitement rippled throughout the crowd. Anna had no doubt of the cause. She looked to the top of the curving marble staircase for confirmation.

Graham and Christine were descending. Christine, her gloved hand resting on the sleeve of Graham's extended arm, was dressed in a low-cut evening gown, accentuating her figure while revealing a good deal of décolletage. Graham was a study in understated elegance in a tuxedo of soft dove gray silk, white tie, white silk brocade vest and tails. Whereas Christine, radiantly beautiful, drew the attention of the majority of those gathered, Anna could not take her eyes off Graham. As they reached the bottom stair, Graham handed Christine down into a crowd of well-wishers, obviously friends Christine had acquired since she and Graham parted. Graham moved away, remarking politely to those who stopped to greet her, yet determined to avoid conversation.

Anna watched her carefully. If you didn't know her, you would not have thought this was her first social gathering since her injury. She looked perfectly composed and entirely in command. Anna, who knew differently, could detect the signs of strain from across the room.

As unobtrusively as possible, she made her way through the crowd to Graham's side.

"Helen is sitting on the divan just to the left of the entrance," Anna said. "I haven't had a chance to talk with her this evening; there have been so many people I don't know. Perhaps you could see me over and pave the way for me?"

"And perhaps rescue myself from the perilous chore of trying to get from here to there on my own?" Graham asked cynically. At Anna's swift intake of breath, Graham realized she had struck out at the wrong person. "You are quite astute, Anna. You seem to have gleaned the obstacles my infirmity presents," she continued self-mockingly. "It would not do to have me stumbling about."

She knew Anna was offering her a way to preserve her dignity without sacrificing her pride, but it had been pride that had gotten her into this situation to begin with. She couldn't bring herself to tell Christine she wouldn't be able to manage in such a large gathering without help. Given enough time to familiarize herself with an area, she could accomplish an astounding degree of independence. With the workers in and out of the dining area and ballroom all week, there simply hadn't been the opportunity. Now she could not safely move about on her own. Christine dealt with the fact of Graham's sightlessness by ignoring it, and had not considered what the evening would demand of her. She had no doubt that Christine would have been solicitous of her every need, and by allowing that Graham would have been diminished in her own eyes, if not that of every person there. She was furious with herself for allowing this to happen.

Anna, stressed herself from the pressures of the evening as well as the constant visage of Graham and Christine everywhere she turned, didn't even try to control her anger. "You are the *least* infirm person I know," she seethed. "What you are is too damn pig-headed for your own good. *Everyone* has some kind of need, Graham—once in a while. Are you so self-sufficient that you consider yourself above that?"

Graham's only response was to raise one elegant eyebrow. "Clearly I have done something to offend you. Whatever that might be, I sincerely apologize. As to the question of my needs, Ms. Reid, let me assure you they are not a matter for discussion."

"Then you can find your own damn way across the room!" Anna snarled. "I'm too tired to argue with you when you're in one of these stubborn, insufferably arrogant moods."

Graham caught Anna's hand as Anna was about to turn away. Anna stared in amazement at the fingers lightly grasping hers. *How on earth does she do that?*

"Now is not the time to discuss my moods or your opinion of them. I don't want to argue with you, nor do I wish to offend you further. I would, however, be honored to escort you to the reception line, and to dinner," Graham continued as if Anna hadn't just railed at her in a tone of voice no one else had ever dared use.

Graham offered her arm, trying to hide her tension and her increasing disorientation as people pressed around them. After a moment's hesitation, Anna slipped her fingers around Graham's forearm.

"What about Christine?" Anna asked as she and Graham made their way across the room.

Graham was exquisitely sensitive to the pressure of Anna's hand, and had no trouble guiding them through the crowd from the faint cues Anna transmitted through her touch. From the first time Anna had taken her arm as they walked through the gardens, there had been that effortless communication. She doubted that Anna even realized the extent to which she provided Graham with a sense of her surroundings.

"Christine has never lacked for escorts at these affairs. She'll soon have some young woman—or man—enthralled. You need have no concern about her."

Anna wasn't so sure as she caught Christine's angry glance at them from where she stood regaling a group of admirers.

The meal, a sumptuous affair replete with culinary delicacies, a bevy of elegant wines, and outrageously decadent desserts, passed uneventfully. Helen was thoroughly enjoying herself. She couldn't wait to usher everyone into the ballroom where a string quartet was waiting to provide the music. Graham had made it clear there was to be no piano in the room. Helen laughed with delight when Graham asked her if she would like to have the first dance with her.

"Oh my goodness, no. You are much too tall for me and far too good a dancer. I'd much rather watch you dance," she cried fondly.

"I think not, Helen," Graham replied flatly.

"You must dance with Anna at least, Graham," Helen chided.

"It's only proper that you do. She is here at your request, after all, and unescorted. Besides, she looks so lovely tonight."

"Does she?" Graham murmured, thinking of the last time she had danced. It had been with Christine at the reception following what was to be her last concert. To her surprise, she couldn't remember what it had felt like.

"Oh yes," Helen enthused. "She has done something with her hair. It's pinned up in some way, and it shows off her face so nicely. She has beautiful cheekbones, rather like a model. She's a golden tan from the sun, and seems to glow naturally. To my mind she's one of the most beautiful women here."

"What color is her dress?" Graham asked almost against her will.

"A deep blue, like her eyes, and it's cut down off her shoulders in a—well, I wouldn't exactly say it's revealing, but she does have an attractive figure."

"Where is she?" Graham brought herself to ask.

"Just inside the door—to your right. And there's no one nearby, if you were to walk directly there from here," Helen added as if it were an afterthought. She knew better than anyone what it took for Graham to make this appearance tonight, and what it required for her to preserve her pride.

"Thank you, Helen," Graham said as she bent to kiss her softly on the cheek.

Helen held her breath as she watched Graham make her way toward Anna. She needn't have worried. Graham's instinct was unerring. Within a moment she was at Anna's side. The orchestra was just beginning the opening waltz.

"Would you honor me with this dance?" Graham asked as she offered her hand to Anna with a slight bow.

Anna was nearly speechless. She had never danced with a woman before, and to dance with Graham, alone, in front of all these people. "Surely Christine will expect this dance," was all she could manage.

Graham straightened, a flicker of ire crossing her fine features. "Christine is neither mistress of this house nor of me. It is not for her to decide. Now *will* you give me this dance?"

The guests who ringed the room receded from Anna's view. All she could see was the woman before her, hand outstretched, waiting. Yardley's master was imperiously commanding, handsome beyond description, and intently focused on Anna. She could no more have denied her than she could have stopped her own heartbeat.

"Yes," Anna said softly, taking the elegant hand. "I'd love to."

Graham made it impossible to be nervous. She danced with the same grace and fluidity with which she played. When Anna stepped into her arms, she knew only gently swirling motion and the warmth of Graham's body against her. She was unaware of those watching but she was acutely aware of every facet of Graham's presence. She felt the rise of Graham's chest against her own breasts, the faint pressure of Graham's thigh against her leg, and the possessive press of Graham's hand on her back. She had never felt so intimately connected to anyone in her life. The sensations slowly coalesced into an ache of desire.

"You're shaking," Graham murmured.

Anna laughed unsteadily against Graham's shoulder, praying her arousal wasn't so obvious. "I think it's nerves. Just don't let go of me."

Graham bent her head until her lips brushed the hair at Anna's temple. "I wouldn't dream of it," she whispered. She drew her close, and their bodies moved effortlessly together.

Christine watched them dance. They fit together well—too well. Graham held Anna protectively within the circle of her arms, her cheek nestled against Anna's fair hair. Anna's eyes were closed, her left hand softly, unconsciously, stroking the stray wisps of Graham's unruly black mane where it brushed against her collar. She trembled visibly, and Christine knew perfectly well why. She had felt the power of Graham's presence herself, and knew what it was to melt with desire in her arms. Anna and Graham melded to one another like lovers, although she was certain Graham had not yet conceived of it. Might never accept it. But Christine had no intention of leaving that up to fate. When the dance ended she intended to reassert her claim on the errant master of Yardley Manor.

Anna was the first one in the household awake the next morning. She was glad she wouldn't have to face anyone, not even Helen. She doubted that she would have been able to hide her feelings under any circumstances. Last night's events were still too fresh, and her anger too potent.

The dance with Graham had literally left her gasping. When at last other couples began to join them, Graham quickly steered them off the floor and out onto the balcony that extended along one entire side of the ballroom. They walked to the railing and stood side-by-side facing the night, their hands nearly touching on the topsail. Candles in glass holders, set strategically on small wrought iron tables, cast a dim light over the area behind them, leaving them in shadow. Only the pale light of the moon illuminated their features.

"You're a wonderful dancer," Anna managed when at last she could control her breathing. She glanced at Graham, who appeared lost in thought. After a long pause Graham seemed to have heard the remark. She smiled faintly.

"Thank you. You are easy to lead," she said. After some hesitation, she continued. "And you are also easy to follow. I must apologize for my 'pig-headed' behavior earlier this evening. You were right in surmising that I needed help." She sighed, a wordless admission of frustration and anger. "I couldn't bring myself to ask. There was a time, Anna, when the world was mine to command, and no one ever suggested otherwise. Now, I continue as if I were still that person—stubborn arrogance I think you said."

It was clearly a struggle for her to admit this much, and Anna had no need for her to humble herself. "It's all right, Graham," she interrupted her quietly. "I can't begin to imagine how difficult this evening must have been. It pleased me to help in some small way. Besides, if you weren't so stubborn, I probably wouldn't—" She stopped abruptly, embarrassed by what she had been about to say. She was rapidly losing all semblance of control around this woman. There was no denying what had happened to her as they danced, what was happening to her now. Graham's nearness aroused her in a way she had never known. She had wanted Graham to touch her so much she was afraid the entire room would know. All she wanted now was to be in her arms again.

Graham tilted her head, waiting for the words that didn't come. She sensed Anna's hesitation, and thought her still offended. She had no way of knowing Anna was struggling to keep from caressing her.

"What is it?" she asked as the silence lengthened. "Anna, have I made you that angry?"

Graham flinched in surprise when Anna stepped closer, placing her hands on Graham's shirtfront. She had known as they danced that she was on dangerous ground. The feel of Anna in her arms had awakened her senses. She had allowed herself the brief touch of her lips to Anna's temple. What she had wanted was to claim her mouth. Anna's hands on her now rekindled desire so long buried it was almost painful to experience. She caught her breath at the paroxysm of arousal, clenching her jaw against the swift burning spasm.

"You've a stud that's come loose," Anna whispered throatily, lifting the edges of Graham's starched shirtfront. She shivered as Graham's hands came to her waist. She fastened the small diamond stud with trembling fingers, so close now that their entire bodies touched lightly. Graham's body rippled with tension, and her grip on Anna tightened. Anna slid her fingers up to Graham's collar, her vision suddenly cloudy. "And your tie needs straightening." She gasped as her breasts, swollen with desire, brushed against Graham's chest.

"Oh God," Anna whispered as Graham drew her slowly nearer until she was pressed tightly to Graham's thigh. She lifted her eyes finally to Graham's and saw raw hunger in her face. Anna needed her kiss like she needed air to breath. She thought she might die with wanting. She slid her hand to the back of Graham's neck, willing her lips closer.

"Please," she implored.

"Anna," Graham murmured thickly, knowing this was wrong, unable to stop. In another moment she would be beyond caring, she would have to have her. She was seconds away from committing the biggest error of her life when a voice from the past called her irrevocably back to reality.

"Graham, darling." Christine stated calmly, as if she hadn't just found her in a passionate embrace with another woman. "I know you hate these affairs, but you simply must be civilized about it. You cannot disappear and deprive us all of your company."

Graham straightened slowly, stepping away from Anna. She spoke into the darkness, her voice cold as ice. "You seem to have managed without my company for quite some time, my dear."

"And more the fool am I," Christine replied as she stepped to Graham's side. She pointedly ignored Anna, who was watching Graham in stunned bewilderment. "I have every intention of making it up to you. Now stop being such a cad, and take me back to the party."

As she spoke, she slipped one arm about Graham's waist, unabashedly caressing her with the other, sliding her hand up the length of Graham's thigh as she pressed against her. Graham grasped the hand that stroked her, but she did not pull away. Instead, she turned to Anna, her face remote.

"Forgive me, Anna, it seems I have obligations to attend to. Good night."

Anna collapsed against the railing, shaking, dazed by Graham's departure. Her body was wracked with hunger for a woman who could arouse her with a glance, and then leave her without a second thought. She had come within a whisper of humiliating herself tonight, and yet—Graham *had* responded, hadn't she?

Anna slammed the cabinet door as the question that had haunted her all night echoed in her mind. What did it matter if Graham had responded? What would it have mattered if she'd actually kissed her? The fact that Graham was aroused by a woman who was obviously trying to seduce her proved nothing. What mattered was that it took only a word from Christine and Graham forgot everything else. How many times, in how many ways, did she need to have that made clear?

"I'm going down to clear the brush from around the lower fountain," she growled as Helen joined her in the kitchen around seven-thirty. "I won't be up for lunch."

Helen stared after her in confusion. She had just run into Graham coming out of her study, and she had snarled at Helen's cheery good morning. What had happened to every one overnight?

As it turned out, Anna was forced to abandon her work early that afternoon. A storm blew up unexpectedly, as was wont to happen on the Cape in summer. Carrying her tools up to the garden shed, she saw Christine and Graham on the rear terrace. The wind was gusting too hard for Anna to hear their conversation, but Christine was obviously upset. She grasped Graham's arm, pressing close to her. Anna had no desire to witness any more of their private moments. She was about to turn away when Graham, looking gravely serious, bent her head and kissed Christine. Christine clung to her, pulling Graham's willowy figure even closer, fervently returning the kiss. Anna did turn from them then; she needed no further proof of Christine's hold on Graham.

"I won't be down for dinner tonight, Helen," she said when she found Helen in the laundry room. "I—I have some work I need to finish."

"Aren't you feeling well?" Helen asked in concern. "Has something happened?" She was well aware of the changes in Anna since Christine had arrived. She was quiet and reclusive, clearly unhappy. Helen hadn't wanted to intrude, but she was becoming more and more worried, about both Anna and Graham. Despite Christine's constant attention, Graham was restrained and brooding. And it hadn't escaped Helen's attention that Graham absolutely refused to play for Christine. Graham was walking the grounds late at night again, a sure sign that she was troubled. And now, Anna too.

"I'm really fine," Anna said, forcing a light tone. "I just— can't. Not tonight."

Helen watched her retreating figure as she hurried from the room and wondered if those hadn't been tears on her cheeks.

Alone in her room, Anna stood for hours looking out over the sea. She struggled to make sense of her confused emotions, but the images of Graham and Christine were all she could envision. She knew she couldn't watch them together day after day. It was too painful, finally more painful than the alternative. Perhaps if last night had never happened she could have learned to live with the reality of Graham loving someone else. Maybe with time, seeing her, but always being apart from her, wouldn't tear her heart out. That was impossible now. Being in her arms last night had changed everything. Their skin may have been separated by the convention of clothing, but what the sheer force of Graham's embrace had evoked was irreversible. She had known the length of Graham's body against hers, had stroked the coiled muscles of her back, and felt the heat of her leg between her own. She would never be able to deny her longing, or control her desire, or tolerate the sight of Christine in Graham's arms. She was not so big a fool as to believe she could stand that. Just as she reached the only decision open to her, a knock sounded on her door.

"Anna? It's Graham. May I come in?"

Anna wiped the tears from her eyes, struggling to compose herself. "Hello," she said softly as she opened the door.

Graham looked concerned. "Are you all right? Helen said not to expect you for dinner."

"Yes. I'm fine."

"I see," Graham replied. She gestured with her hand. "May I come in?"

"Of course." Anna remained standing, too restless to sit.

Graham sensed Anna's distress, and worried she was the cause of it. She had agonized over her lapse the evening before, finally leaving the gathering over Christine's protests to spend the night pacing in her study. She had overstepped her bounds, and she had no excuse for it. For a brief moment she had forgotten everything—the loss of her sight, the loss of Christine, even the loss of her music—all had faded until there was only Anna. Anna in her arms, breathing life into her with her desire. She had succumbed to the physical demands of her body, and God only knew what she might have done if Christine hadn't interrupted them. She had been perilously close to making love to Anna right there on the balcony. The vestiges of arousal lingered throughout the night, and even now, with Anna near, she struggled to maintain her distance. She had hoped Anna might overlook her indiscretion, but now she wasn't sure. "What is it, Anna?" she asked seriously.

Anna spoke the painful words before she lost courage. "Graham, I've been meaning to speak with you for some time. I've decided to move back to the city."

Graham's head jerked as if she had been slapped, feeling the words like a physical blow. Her face drained of color. "But why?" she gasped. Her chest ached, and she struggled for breath. "Is it because of my behavior last night? Anna? I have no excuse—I'm sorry, I—what can I say? It won't happen again, you have my word. Please believe me."

Anna laughed at the bitter irony. "I do believe you. It's not about last night, and if it were, I should be the one to apologize."

"Then what for God's sake?" Graham demanded, her voice hoarse with strain.

Anna looked away, unable to face Graham's suffering. She knew her resolve would weaken if she saw Graham in pain. "I need to be closer to the university, and I'm—"

She's young and she wants a life, you fool! Graham stopped her, unable to stand the crushing truth. "You don't need to explain," she said harshly. "This is no life for you here, isolated on this godforsaken pinnacle of forgotten land. I understand. Of course you must leave."

Anna wanted to scream. *No you don't understand! But how can I tell you that I can't stand to see you with Christine? How can I say 'I love you' when I know it will only drive you away.* Graham looked so vulnerable, Anna bit her lip to keep back the words. She longed to bring the smile back to Graham's face, to stroke the lines from her brow. She wanted to fling herself into her arms. Oh God. Must she really leave?

Graham summoned every ounce of her formidable will, forcing the pain into the recesses of her soul. That was something she had grown used to doing, and now it served her well. She would not let Anna know this was destroying her; she would save her pride.

"Christine will be leaving tomorrow. Can you stay until I arrange some business affairs?" Graham's tone was empty of any emotion, and her expression revealed nothing of her inner despair. She had expected this, but now that it had happened, it was so much worse than she had imagined. For a short time Anna had brought life to this desolate place, to her desolate heart. She had not dared to hope that Anna would stay. Yardley, and all it held within its walls, was dying. It was selfish and foolhardy to think that Anna would have any reason to remain.

"Leaving?" Anna cried. "But I thought—"

Graham looked toward her, a question in her eyes. "You thought what?"

Anna was more confused than ever. She could do nothing save tell the truth. "I thought you and she were lovers. I thought that's why she had come back."

Graham walked to the fireplace, extending one long arm along the mantle, facing the empty grate. "Yes—we were, once. I was twenty-five years old and my whole life was music. I never knew, nor wanted anything more. Oh, I didn't lack for company. There were—dalliances. Usually with women impressed by my reputation. The reality generally proved much less to their liking. Then suddenly Christine entered my life. She was so young, so beautiful, so vital. She showed me a passion that nearly matched my music. I was mad about her, mad for her. But it was my passion, not hers. She never really felt the same, but I refused to see that. I wouldn't believe that my love was more than she wanted, or, as it turned out, not the kind of love she wanted. She tried to tell me that I was too demanding, too possessive—too intense for her, I think she said. I have yet to understand how love can be too intense."

Graham laughed bitterly. "I wouldn't hear what she was trying to tell me. I was so certain of myself. I thought with my music and Christine by my side I had all I needed in this life." She paused, her hand clenched tightly around the mantle's edge. When she spoke again, her voice was tight with pain. "The night of the accident, she told me she was leaving me to marry Richard Blair. I nearly went mad, thinking of her with him—all the time she had been with me. I was wild, raging with jealousy. I swore I wouldn't let her leave me. I frightened her, although God knows I never would have touched her in anger. She tried to jump from the car, and when I grabbed for her I lost control of the wheel. I just managed to pull her under me when we started to roll. The next thing I remember was waking up in the hospital. I heard my father's voice. When I opened my eyes, I knew instantly that I was blind. The darkness was everywhere, but nowhere deeper than in my heart. It was all my fault, you see. I had been too proud and too arrogant to hear that she was unhappy, that she in fact did not share my passion. She did not love me, not really, and I nearly killed her."

Graham's voice broke with the all-too familiar bitter memories. She had almost killed Christine, the woman she swore she loved with all her heart. Losing her sight had seemed like a small price to pay for that sin. And now Anna would be gone too. She tried unsuccessfully to hide the tears that coursed down her cheeks. She fought desperately to seal the anguish away once more. She flinched when Anna brushed the tears from her face.

"Please don't," Graham managed, forcing the words through the pain in her chest. "I didn't mean for you to see this. Please forget it, won't you?"

"I'm so sorry, Graham. I didn't know," Anna whispered tenderly. All thoughts of her own despair dissipated in the face of Graham's agony. "I saw you together in the garden today. I saw you kissing her. I can't believe she could leave you again."

Graham shook her head, not comprehending Anna's words. "I told her today that I had no wish for us to be together again. Anna, I was kissing her good-bye."

Anna could only imagine that Graham was afraid to trust Christine again. Regardless of her own tangled emotions, she had no desire to see Graham suffer any more than she already had.

"Graham, you mustn't be afraid. You can try again. Perhaps you've both changed. It could be different now. You don't have to be alone—"

"Anna," Graham said vehemently, "you don't understand. I don't love Christine—I don't *want* to love her. She has come here to escape her boredom, or to torture her husband with the reminder of our affair, but eventually she would tire of the charade, and she would leave. If I let her stay, it would be a mockery of love. I won't have that." She shook her head fiercely, her voice strident in protest. "No! Christine does not love me. Perhaps she never did."

The words brought both a deep sadness and a curious sense of relief as she spoke them. Exhausted, she sank into the chair, trying to find a way to cope with Anna's leaving. She bowed her head into her hand, too weary to struggle any longer. "I'm sorry. Please excuse my outburst. All of this has been—hard for me. Just give me a moment, then I'll go."

Anna took a deep breath. "Graham, I don't want to leave Yardley. This last month has been difficult, especially when I thought you and Christine were reuniting. I didn't think I'd be needed any longer. But I have been happy here, happier than I have ever been, and I *don't* want to leave."

Graham drew a shuddering breath. "Are you sure?" The eyes she turned to Anna were wounded, nearly devoid of hope. She hadn't the strength to contain her despair, and the sight of it ripped at Anna's heart.

Though her situation with Graham was no clearer, she would at least be spared the sight of Christine every day. And she would be miserable if she left. She couldn't imagine never seeing Graham again. She cupped Graham's face gently in her hands. "I'm very sure. I want to stay."

Graham pressed her lips to Anna's palm, her relief nearly palpable. Only time would tell if Anna had made the right decision.

CHAPTER FOURTEEN

With Christine's departure, a semblance of harmony returned to Yardley. With the end of summer, Anna resumed her classes three days a week, which left more than ample time to manage the household needs and Graham's business requirements. She met with Graham at the end of her day, and more often than not, they merely talked. Graham was keenly interested in Anna's studies, and Anna found herself recounting her days in detail while they shared a glass of sherry. It was something she looked forward to, and it seemed that Graham did as well. Their relationship slowly developed into a comfortable but reserved companionship.

Neither of them made any mention of the episode on the balcony the night of Helen's party. Anna did not know how to broach it, and Graham seemed to avoid any possibility of intimacy. Although she welcomed their conversations, she remained physically remote. She was careful not to touch Anna even when it would have been natural to. Her caution in this regard did not escape Anna's notice, and Anna interpreted it as an unspoken declaration from Graham that their brief physical interlude had been an aberration of circumstance. It had been a tense and stressful period for both of them, and in the intensity of the moment that night, Graham had responded to Anna's overture. Obviously, it was not something Graham wished to repeat.

Anna for her part tried her best to forget what had passed between them, and to content herself with the relationship they were so carefully building. Graham was not so quick to withdraw from her at the slightest mention of her past; in fact, to Anna's amazement, Graham occasionally alluded to some previous event with an ease that was absent a few months before. Graham was beginning to trust her, and for now that appeared to be the most she could hope for. She resigned herself to what they could share together, because she knew in the final analysis, she would be miserable without Graham in her life. She tried not to think of what she would do if all Graham ever wanted from her was this distant friendship.

Perhaps the only person at Yardley who was able to see just what was happening between the two of them was Helen. She knew the extent to which Graham was capable of closing off parts of herself, and of denying her own wants and needs. Graham had deluded herself for years with Christine. Helen wondered if she would be as successful disavowing her feelings for Anna.

When Helen brought tea into Graham late one afternoon, Graham greeted her warmly. She was at work at the piano, as relaxed as Helen had seen her in many years. Helen thought approvingly of how good Graham looked. She was no longer unnaturally pale, nor wraithlike thin. Her lean form was stronger from the time she spent outside. She had taken to joining Helen and Anna most evenings for dinner, and their conversations were light and easy. Helen thought she understood the reason for Graham's emergence from the torpor that had enveloped her, but she wondered if Graham truly did. Helen couldn't help but notice that as Graham grew more peaceful, Anna became more despondent.

"Thank you, Helen," Graham said fondly as she rose from her seat at the piano, stretching gratefully. She felt wonderful. Her world was filled with sound, the way it had been when she was young. Her blood stirred with long-forgotten excitement. She attributed it to the ease with which she was working and the satisfaction that brought her. She refused to admit to herself that Anna's return was the moment she waited for all day.

"You look happy, Graham," Helen remarked.

"Happy?" Graham said, wondering if that was what she felt.

"Yes, perhaps that's it. At any rate, Helen, the music is returning, and that is more than I ever expected to have again in this life."

"I'm happy for you," Helen said, and she truly rejoiced in the change in Graham over the last few months. But she couldn't help but wonder if that was all Graham wanted from life. The passionate woman she had known would never have been content alone. Graham had needed the sustenance of love to balance the soul-draining demands of her work. She had made a disastrous misjudgment in relying on Christine so completely, and she had paid a dreadful price for it. Helen only hoped that that disappointment had not destroyed Graham's ability to accept love when it was offered from the heart.

Anna tossed her knapsack on the hall table, waving to Helen as she headed toward the music room. She knew Graham would be there, as she always was at this time of day. She tapped lightly on the door before entering. Graham lifted one hand, the other poised over the piano keys.

"Just a minute. I've nearly finished."

Anna crossed quietly to stand beside Graham, watching as she played, marveling at the graceful sweep of her fingers on the keys. As her hands literally caressed the instrument, her face reflected all the emotions the music gave form to. The combination of watching Graham's face and hearing her creation stirred Anna unexpectedly. As the notes dissipated in the air, Graham became motionless, her hands lying still on her thighs.

"It's wonderful," Anna breathed softly.

Graham lifted her face to Anna, an uncharacteristic uncertainty clouding her features. "Do you really think so?" she asked quietly.

Sometimes Anna felt as much a prisoner of Graham's blindness as Graham certainly was. She felt so much more than her words could communicate, and she wished that Graham could read in her face how deeply she was moved. Graham's music could bring her to tears. She knew that from standing outside this room, stilled in mid-step by what she heard, and because she had sought out the recordings Graham had made years before. She played them when she was alone, imagining Graham's face as she listened. For her, nothing was more heart-rending than watching Graham play, raw passions exposed, as the music swirled in the air. For Graham not to see what she was capable of stirring in others pierced Anna's heart.

Instinctively, she placed both hands gently on Graham's shoulders, leaning over to whisper, "It makes me ache. Will you play it for me from the beginning?" She had never asked before.

Graham reached up to cover Anna's hand with her own, surprised once again by the warmth of her skin. She lingered like that for a moment, then settled her hands on the keys.

"Yes."

Anna moved reluctantly away, not wanting to dispel that rare moment of affection. Still, she knew Graham had taken another step toward allowing Anna into her life. Graham had not allowed anyone to hear more than fragments of a work in progress for years.

Anna settled into a nearby chair from which she could watch Graham play. She found herself holding her breath as the melody swelled to fill the air. She would not have believed that there could be such a thing as too much beauty, but the sight and sounds of Graham Yardley overwhelmed her. She closed her eyes and let the golden tones carry her away. When the room stilled, it took her a moment to find her composure. She was trembling, and her voice seemed to have deserted her. When she opened her eyes, she found that Graham had turned to face her, her head bent, waiting.

"I've never imagined anything so exquisite," Anna said quietly. "Your music is a gift to the world, Graham. Thank you so much for sharing it with me."

Graham lifted her head, her face wet with tears. "I thought it was gone forever," she murmured, her voice breaking.

The sight of her tears was Anna's undoing. She meant only to take Graham's hand in hers, but she found herself pulling Graham up into her arms instead. She held her close, whispering, "Oh God, Graham— your music breaks my heart. *You* break my heart."

Graham struggled with the response Anna's embrace wrought. Anna's body was pressed to hers; she felt the rise and fall of Anna's soft breasts with each breath; their hearts seemed to race as one. Anna's nearness, and her words, filled her with a longing so intense her carefully maintained barricades threatened to crumble. And she feared that if she gave rein to her emotions, she would be captive to them as she had been with Christine. She knew she could not survive another disappointment. If ever such pain returned anew, she would surely break. What Anna touched in her was a place too dangerous to expose. For the sake of whatever sanity she had left, she could not let that happen.

Anna felt Graham stiffen, but she only pulled her tighter. Was there no way for Anna to show her how precious she was? "You are so rare. There is such grace and beauty and tenderness in your soul. And you don't even know it, do you? You're so special—I can't begin to tell you—" She had no words, only sensations. Admiration, respect, protectiveness, sympathy, and sweet, swift longing. Everything condensed at once until Anna had to give form to her feelings or explode. Her hands moved from Graham's back to cup her jaw, then slid into her hair as she groaned softly, "If only I could tell you—" Her lips met Graham's as the words escaped her in a rush.

Graham gasped at the contact, her control all but shattered. For an instant she knew only the wellspring of desire that rippled through her, the moist heat that flooded from her. With a groan she opened herself to the raging fire, embracing its source. Even as she pulled Anna roughly to her, giving herself fully to the kiss, a suffocating dread began to eclipse her passion. She felt more vulnerable than she had during the first seconds of her blindness, when she opened her eyes to a darkness more terrifying than anything she had ever experienced. *This* was what she truly had isolated herself from all these years—this horrible power that love wielded over her.

"Anna, no—" Graham rasped, catching the hands that brushed down her shirtfront toward her breasts. She grasped Anna's wrists softly, gently disengaging from their embrace. She struggled for air for an instant, her brain whirling, then finally managed to whisper hoarsely, "You honor me, Anna. With your appreciation, with your deep kindness. I am only too glad to give you what I can with my music. That it pleases you means more to me than I can say. But that is all I can give, Anna— I'm sorry."

Graham's withdrawal was like a knife slashing through Anna's depths. Must she always be left with this terrible emptiness? She didn't want to let her go, but she knew she must. She could not force Graham to feel as she felt, to want what she wanted.

"No, I'm sorry," she replied shakily. "I can't seem to stop throwing myself at you. You've made it perfectly clear—"

"Anna, don't," Graham murmured. "There is no need for an apology."

Anna drew a long breath, steadying herself. When she spoke again her voice had a steely calm. "Thank you, Graham, for trusting me with your music. It meant more to me than I can ever say." She turned to leave, but couldn't help but ask, "Will I see you at dinner?"

Graham shook her head, "Not tonight, Anna."

"Is Graham coming for dinner?" Helen asked as she set out the hot rolls to cool.

Anna shook her head, busying herself with the dishes. She didn't trust herself to speak, she was still shaking.

"Working still, is she?"

"Yes," Anna managed.

Helen gave her a concerned look. The girl was completely white. "Everything going all right?" she asked cautiously.

"She finished something this afternoon," Anna replied hollowly. After a pause, she added softly, "It was unbelievable."

"Oh?" Helen asked in surprise. "She played it for you?"

"Yes, she did," Anna replied, her voice devoid of emotion. Helen gave Anna her full attention, setting aside the roast she was carving. For Graham to have played for Anna was nothing short of a miracle, but it seemed to have produced anything but a happy response.

"Graham can be very self-absorbed when she's working. Sometimes she forgets about common civility and other people's feelings," she ventured, thinking that Graham's notoriously volatile nature may have given offense.

"She was perfectly charming, as always," Anna remarked somewhat harshly. Graham raised even rejection to an art form. *Damn her pristine control! Isn't there anything that moves her?* Anna was only too afraid she knew the answer to that.

"Well, she's done something, now hasn't she?" Helen persisted softly.

"No, Helen," Anna began, surrendering to her frustration. "*I've* done something." *I've fallen in love with her*. She closed her eyes, searching for calm. She couldn't very well tell Helen that she wanted Graham to make love to her, now could she? "I can't seem to reach her," she said carefully. "She is always polite, always cordial and her distance is driving me crazy. She won't accept one compliment; she can't hear one kind word, without mistrusting it. It's so hard when you care about her." She caught back a sob, struggling for the tatters of her own self-control.

"Graham has been alone a very long time," Helen said carefully. "She has forgotten how to get on with people." She sensed it was more serious than that, but Helen didn't want to embarrass Anna if her assumptions were wrong. Anna's moodiness hadn't escaped her notice, and neither had Graham's growing reliance on the younger woman. She had been expecting some kind of confrontation for weeks.

"Well, she certainly seemed to know how to get along with Christine," Anna said angrily. *She certainly didn't have any problems kissing her*, she wanted to shout. *Oh God, I really am losing my mind.*

"Christine?" Helen responded dismissively. "Graham suffered her presence, that's all."

"I'm not so sure about that," Anna responded, her anger escalating, too hurt for caution. "She suffered a lot more than her *presence*. She allowed that woman to fall all over her, and she could deny her nothing. I think she's still in love with her and is just too damn stubborn to admit it."

"So she told you about them, did she?" Helen asked, beginning to get a better idea about the source of Anna's distress.

"Yes, she told me!" Anna barked. "The love affair to end all love affairs. Whether Christine is here or not, she will always have that hold on Graham. God, I'm such a fool."

Helen shook her head adamantly, "Oh no, my dear. You are wrong. Graham made a fool out of herself over that girl, but she wasn't so much a fool that she would do it twice. When Christine left Graham for Richard Blair, she not only broke Graham's heart, she betrayed everything Graham believed love to be. As hard as it was, at some point even Graham had to accept that she was only an exciting and forbidden diversion for Christine. Love her still? No my dear, Graham would never have forgiven the betrayal."

"Then what is it that keeps her so apart?" Anna beseeched. "She is so talented, so sensitive, so kind. How can she bury all of that as if it meant nothing? As if she herself meant nothing? What is she hiding from?"

Helen had never seen Anna so distraught, and she knew the only words that might help her would also reveal Graham's deepest secrets. It was not for her to expose Graham in that way.

"Perhaps she just needs time, Anna. These last months, since you've come, she's changed so much. Oh, I know you can't see it—but I can. She no longer sits for hours, alone in her rooms, or wanders the bluff at all hours of the night. There is life in her now, Anna, life that has been missing for more than a decade. Just listen to her music if you don't believe me. You led her back into the world. You put a flower in her hand and showed her there was life that she could experience still. Such a simple thing as a flower; it took you to do that."

Anna shook her head, feeling sad and defeated. "Whatever else she needs, I can't seem to give her. And I don't know how much more

I can take." She looked at Helen with despair in her eyes. "I'm sorry, Helen, you don't deserve this. I don't even know why I'm so upset—I don't even know what I'm feeling half the time. It's foolish of me to be carrying on like this. Maybe I'm just being selfish. Graham certainly seems content." She gave Helen a tremulous smile and a swift hug. "Don't wait dinner for me," she said as she hurried from the room.

Helen looked after her, conflicting loyalties warring in her mind. As much as she adored Graham Yardley, she couldn't stand by and watch Anna suffer.

"Graham?" Helen called at the music room door. She entered to find the room deserted. The doors to the terrace were open, despite the brisk October wind. A few leaves fluttered through and clustered on the floor. Graham's body was outlined in moonlight as she leaned against the balustrade, facing out to the night. Her light shirt whipped about her thin form in the wind.

Helen wrapped her shawl tighter around herself and ventured out. The chill in Graham's fingers shocked her when she covered her hand where it lay on the railing.

"Graham. You're freezing. Come inside."

"I'm fine, Helen," Graham answered hollowly. "Go back— it's too cold here for you."

"And you're made of stone?" Helen snapped, her patience perilously close to gone. First Anna, and now Graham—the two of them suffering was more than she could watch in silence.

"It seems that I am," replied Graham with a cynical smile.

"I know better than that, and you would too if you'd let yourself admit it."

"Helen," Graham said warningly, "I love you like my own parent, but this is something you know nothing about. Let it alone, please—for my sake."

"I have. All these years when you locked yourself away here, I've left you alone. But there's not just you anymore—there's Anna."

"Helen," Graham growled harshly, "leave Anna out of this."

"I would if I could, but that's not up to me, is it? I've watched you dying slowly right before my eyes for too many years—you who I cherish with all my heart, and I've never said a word, never tried to change your mind. I know how much you lost—and your sight was the least of it."

"Helen, please," Graham whispered, her fists clenched against the stone rail, "please, don't do this now. Please let me have some peace."

"This is not peace, Graham. You may be blind, but your heart is not. You may think love deserted you, but you know as well as I do that wasn't love. I won't believe you can't recognize it when you feel it. Anna *loves* you—"

"Anna *pities* me."

"No, Graham. For once your blindness *has* trapped you. I can *see* what you refuse to feel. I only have to look at her looking at you to know. She loves you, Graham."

A groan escaped Graham as she turned away. "You know me Helen. You know what my life demands, what *I* demand. Do you truly think anyone, especially someone as young and vital as Anna, would stay, once she knew what it really meant? I might have killed Christine in the car that night, because she couldn't give me what I wanted. Because she was leaving me. I believed once, and it destroyed me. I will not believe again. I cannot survive the loss."

"You underestimate her, Graham—and it's not just yourself you're hurting now. You're breaking her heart."

"No!" Graham shouted, her fists pounding the unyielding stone. "I cannot, I *will* not, let this happen. It would destroy us both. I will not bind her to this barren world that is my heart. Now leave me, please— I beg of you." Her last words came in a choked whisper, and tears streaked down her anguished face.

Helen bent her head in defeat, longing to take the trembling woman in her arms. But she knew that Graham would not allow even that sympathy. What Graham feared was inside herself, and nothing could assuage her inconsolable grief.

Chapter Fifteen

Silence descended on Yardley Manor as each of them struggled to accept their disappointments. Anna went about her work with quiet resignation, an aching hollowness her constant companion. Whereas once the time she spent with Graham eased her loneliness, now seeing her only seemed to heighten it. And Graham, if possible, was even more remote. They spent less time together, as Graham often absented herself from the music room in the afternoons. Instead she worked late into the night, after the others were asleep. She had begun taking her meals alone again, although the trays came back barely touched. The music that echoed in the corridors was dark and melancholy. The one place Graham could not hide her emotions was in her music. It was truly the mirror of her soul. Helen stood by helplessly, knowing that only Graham could change the course of their lives. Late one evening, to Helen's surprise, Graham came to the door of her sitting room.

"Graham, good gracious," she exclaimed. "What's wrong?"

"Helen," Graham said urgently, without preamble. "Where is Anna?"

Helen glanced at the clock on her mantle. It was almost eleven, and it occurred to her she hadn't seen Anna all evening. "I don't know. She wasn't here for dinner. Hasn't she come up?"

"No, and I haven't heard the Jeep return," Graham remarked, barely able to hide her anxiety. In some part of her consciousness she waited for the day Anna would not return. It was impossible for her to work when Anna wasn't about the house or grounds. She couldn't concentrate, couldn't rest, without knowing she was near. Especially recently, since their estrangement, she found herself listening for Anna's step in the hall or the distinctive crunch of gravel in the drive. As much as she expected Anna to leave, she feared it. When it happened, she would lose whatever small purchase on life she had left.

Helen could read the fear in Graham's face. Ordinarily she wouldn't have worried, but Anna hadn't been herself lately. She often seemed distracted, almost dazed. Helen began to worry that Anna might have had an accident.

It was hard for Helen not to think of that awful night when the call had come about Graham's accident. She remembered only too well the agonizing hour they had all spent while men worked to free her from the wreckage. It was an hour spent not knowing if she were still alive. Helen struggled to dispel the image and quell the surge of alarm. Anna must simply have forgotten to mention her plans. Any other possibility was more than she could bear to contemplate.

She struggled to keep her voice even. "I'm sure she's fine, Graham. Go on to bed. I'll be up. If there's any problem, she'll call."

A look of panic flickered across Graham's face. Helen knew as well as she that Anna never absented herself without word. With effort she said evenly, "Of course, you're right. Just the same, I'll wait in the library in case she calls."

Helen listened to the echo of her retreating steps, losing sight of her as she descended the dark stairway with a measured step. She knew Graham was every bit as stretched to the limit as Anna seemed to be. She wondered fearfully which one of them would lose the thin rein of control first.

The hallway was dark when Anna let herself into the house just after one in the morning. She jumped when a voice called out to her.

"Anna?"

Anna fumbled for the light switch as she stepped into the library. Graham was seated in a chair before the window that fronted the main drive, as she had been for hours.

"Graham?" Anna asked in surprise "What are you doing in here?"

"We were worried—Helen and I. I was waiting in case you called." Graham rose, and began to pace restlessly. "Although God knows what I thought I could do about it if you were in trouble," she laughed bitterly. "We make a fine pair, Helen and I. One who can't drive, and the other one blind."

"Oh God, Graham," Anna cried. "I stayed to have dinner with my graduate advisor. It wasn't planned. I should have called, but we started talking and I lost track of the time." She felt miserable for having worried either of them.

Graham made an impatient gesture, infuriated with her helplessness, embarrassed by her near panic. "Nonsense. You don't owe either of us an explanation. Your private life is none of our affair. Where you spend your time—and with whom, does not concern us."

Anna gaped at her. Graham Yardley had to be the most infuriating woman she had ever met. "Is that what you think? That I was out on a *date* for God's sake?"

Graham straightened her shoulders, anger replacing her worry. There was no need for Anna to know she had spent several anxious hours fearing she had left for good. "I don't think anything one way or the other, nor do I care. As I said—"

"I know damn well what you *said*, Graham," Anna seethed, absolutely beyond caring whether she offended Graham or not. "What I don't understand is why you said it. You know very well how I feel about you, whether you choose to acknowledge it or not. I've done everything short of begging you. Don't insult me by suggesting I would simply wander off and find consolation elsewhere. Do you think you're the only one capable of a true and honorable emotion? Damn your arrogance!"

"It was not my intention to insult you, Anna," Graham replied in an amazingly calm tone. She couldn't remember the last time someone raised their voice to her, other than Christine. Anna's sincere distress had a greater effect on her than Christine's tirades ever had. "I did not mean for us to come to this," she said softly. "I never meant to misrepresent myself to you in any way."

"Don't worry, Graham. You haven't," Anna snapped. "I'm the one who's been mistaken, but I assure you, I will not trouble you again." She grabbed her knapsack, intent on retreating before she completely lost the last vestige of restraint. She had tried so hard to be patient, to accept the depth of Graham's loss and disappointment, but it hadn't made any difference and she doubted it ever would.

"I have legal matters that require your assistance. I'll need to meet with you tomorrow," Graham said as Anna stepped out into the hall. She hated this animosity between them, but there seemed no other way.

"Certainly," Anna rejoined coldly. "I'll see you in the afternoon."

Anna left her there, but she could not bring herself to turn out the light, even though the darkness would not matter to Graham.

Anna worked furiously, digging up buried roots with a spade, slashing through briars with a machete, flinging clods of earth aside with a vengeance. Her pace matched her mood. She was still boiling. She wasn't sure with whom she was angrier—Graham or herself. What had she expected? Graham Yardley was a wealthy, gifted woman who had known both fame and great passion in her life. Under any circumstances she would hardly be expected to notice someone like Anna, and now, after all she had suffered, she had no special feeling for Anna.

Anna struggled for acceptance, but it was so hard. What she felt for Graham went so far beyond anything she had experienced, or dreamed of experiencing. The wanting surpassed simple desire—she felt inextricably linked to her, body and soul. When she saw Graham across the room, when the sound of her voice carried out into the garden, when she heard her piano whisper in the night, fire surged through her being. Some primal part of her had been called to life by this woman. The combination of Graham's great strength and her great need had awakened Anna's deepest passion. To be near her, and so apart, was unendurable. She was beginning to contemplate the unthinkable. She might need to leave Yardley. She didn't have the strength to subjugate her desires to reason. She simply couldn't be around Graham and not want her. For a few months she had managed to be content with their carefully contained relationship, but since the instant they had kissed, all that had changed. She couldn't forget it, and she couldn't stop wanting it again. She would lose her mind if she stayed, and if she left she would lose her soul. It was a choice that was no choice at all, and she cursed her own indecisiveness under her breath. She rubbed the tears from her face and grabbed her ax. She intended to cut down every dead limb at Yardley before the day was out.

While Anna warred with her emotions amidst the tangled undergrowth, Graham paced the flagstone terrace fighting her own demons. She knew she was hurting Anna by refusing to acknowledge what was between them, and she had no answer for it. Anna had restored life to Yardley, and to her. With Anna had come the scent of fresh flowers and the teasing sound of notes in the air. Graham had responded to both as if light had suddenly been returned to her world. Her heart lifted to the sounds of Anna's footsteps in the hall. Anna's presence had muted the pain of years of loneliness. But Anna had awakened other senses as well. Graham knew the touch of her hands, the warmth of her skin, the soft fullness of her breasts. She knew the bruising demand of Anna's kiss as her lips searched against Graham's mouth. If she made love to her, she would have to acknowledge what was in her heart. If she gave freedom to everything Anna ignited in her, she would never be able to live without her. That was what Graham retreated from. She dared not entrust her soul again, and she could not love any other way. They sat thus, separated not by distance, but by uncertainty.

Anna sighed and stepped back from the line of trees she had been pruning. She could hear the delicate strains of Graham's music wafting on the breeze. She glanced up at the sky, noting absently that clouds were amassing out over the ocean. She reached for her worn denim work jacket as the sudden wind off the water brought a brisk chill to the air. She didn't want to return to the house yet; she still felt too unsettled. She needed to fortify herself before she joined Graham in her music room for their late afternoon meeting.

Graham looked up from the keyboard as the curtains floated into the room on a chill breeze. The weight of the air on her face was dense and wet. Something ominous was stirring, and one word clamored in her mind—*Anna*. She bolted up from the piano bench in a rush, pushing the terrace doors wide as she stormed through them. From the top of the stairs leading down the flagstone path to the lower reaches of the property, she called out into the gathering wind.

"Anna!"

Anna looked up at the sound of Graham's voice, amazed to see the sky blackening around her. The rain and heavy winds were upon her before she knew it. In an instant a blinding wall of water blew in from the sea, drenching her and turning the garden path into a hundred yards of steep, slippery mud. To her horror she saw Graham start down toward her.

"Graham! No, go back!" she cried, paralyzed with fear at the thought of Graham exposed in the storm. "Go back. I'm coming up."

Abandoning her tools, Anna began to climb the path, struggling to keep her balance in the buffeting winds and pounding rain. Tree branches bent and broke in the wind, hurtling by in the swirling gale. Lightening flashed around her, and the house seemed impossibly far away. She heard a tremendous crash to her left and knew, even as she knew she could not move quickly enough to avoid it, that the old sycamore had been struck by lightening. She threw up an arm to shield her face and cried out as falling branches and limbs engulfed her. There was an instant of white-hot pain in her shoulder just as she met the ground with a jarring thud.

Her first sensation after the initial shock was of the penetrating cold that encompassed her. The ground beneath her cheek was sodden, and her denim jeans and shirt clung to her clammy skin. The cold was almost instantly replaced with a stabbing pain in her left side and a throbbing ache in the back of her head. Her next thought was even more terrifying. Where was Graham? *Oh my God! She's out in this storm alone!* She pushed at the overlying branches holding her captive, managing only to worsen the pain in her arm. She fought against the need to vomit, finally ceasing her ineffective struggles. She dropped her head back to the wet ground and waited for the nausea to subside. Time seemed to slow as water dripped through the fallen tree's leaves onto her face. At some point through her disorientation she thought she could hear voices.

"For God's sake man, hurry!"

Anna recognized Graham's deep voice, harsh with fear. Anna struggled to call Graham's name, to tell her she was all right, but all that emerged was a faint groan. *She shouldn't be out here*, she thought hysterically.

"Graham," she finally croaked. "Be careful."

"Anna—thank God!" Graham shouted, her voice choked with anxiety. "Are you hurt, love?"

"I don't think so," Anna said as steadily as she could. In truth she was more worried about Graham than she was about her own scrapes and bruises. "Go inside—call someone to help. Please Graham, please don't stay out here. Go back to the house. Just do it for me."

"Damn if I will. We'll have you free in a moment. Just hang on, Anna." Graham called from somewhere quite close. "Damn it, John, can't you go any faster?" She pulled at the tree limbs in front of her, nearly mad with frustration at her inability to reach Anna. She was impervious to the branches that slashed at her hands and face. God, how she hated her blindness.

"I almost have the limb free, ma'am, but it would help if you'd move back. We don't need both of you under this damn tree."

Graham turned angry eyes toward the man beside her and growled, "I'm not moving until you get her out."

A tremendous creak accompanied the shifting of the huge fork of limb that imprisoned Anna, and she cried out as the weight of the tree shifted off her tender body. Suddenly Graham was beside her, reaching a tentative, trembling hand toward her.

"Don't move," Graham whispered softly, "you're safe now. John will have the rest of it off in a minute."

Graham settled on the muddy slope, unmindful of the water or the cold, and very gently lifted Anna's head into her lap. Despite her pain, Anna lifted both arms around Graham's neck, pressing her face against her chest.

"I'm so glad you're here," Anna whispered, clutching her tightly.

"I'll not leave you," Graham replied, struggling to contain tears. She rocked Anna tenderly as she buried her face in Anna's damp hair. "I'm here."

Anna scarcely felt any pain as she thrilled to the comfort of Graham's presence. As more of the tree was removed she tried moving her legs. Everything worked but she gasped as a multitude of small cuts began to burn.

"Where are you hurt?" Graham asked when she had control of herself again.

"My shoulder, but I don't think anything's broken." Anna began to realize that both of them were shivering nearly uncontrollably. "Graham," she chattered, "you have to get inside. Let me stand up."

"We'd better wait for the doctor. And I'm not leaving you." Graham swore inwardly at her own helplessness, even as she began to believe Anna was safe. For a few agonizing minutes she had feared she had lost her. She heard the tree cracking and Anna's cry as it fell. Helen had confirmed her fear that Anna had been trapped under the downed tree, and the panic that followed almost proved to be Graham's undoing. All she could think of was that Anna was gone, a realization so painful she thought she would go mad. It was Helen who had the presence of mind to call both the family doctor as well as an old friend who lived nearby for help. She couldn't stop Graham from rushing headlong down the treacherous path, only to be unable to find Anna in the tangle of branches, flailing with anguished despair at obstacles she couldn't see. Helen feared that Graham would do herself real harm in her rage to find the girl.

Even with Anna in her arms, Graham was afraid to loosen her hold. Her hands ceaselessly roamed over Anna's body, seeking reassurance that Anna was safe. She didn't realize that each shaking breath bordered on a sob. She hadn't felt such panic since the night of the car crash, when she drifted in and out of consciousness, calling for Christine, getting no answer. She had lain in the twisted wreckage blinded by the blood in her eyes, trapped by the metal that pierced her leg, wondering frantically if she had killed Christine in her jealous rage. Had that been true, in all likelihood she would have taken her own life. Tonight, for those agonizing minutes before she heard Anna's voice, she thought that all that remained to her of life had been taken. Her relief was so enormous, she acted without thinking. She raised Anna's head with a hand cupped to her chin, capturing her mouth with a deep groan.

Oblivious to all else, Anna returned her kiss with a hunger long denied. She gasped when Graham pulled away with a shaky laugh.

"We can't wait any longer, Anna. You're hurt and cold. We must get you inside." Raising her head, but maintaining her fierce hold on the woman in her arms, she called out, "John, help me to get her up."

A tall man pulled the last of the debris free and moved through the darkness to their side. He carefully lifted Anna to her feet. Graham rose unsteadily beside them, her hand clasped in Anna's. Together they made their way slowly back to Yardley Manor.

CHAPTER SIXTEEN

The doctor closed Anna's door gently and nearly collided with Graham where she stood pacing in the hallway. At the soft sound of the latch catching, Graham turned abruptly, her dark eyes shadowed with anxiety.

"How is she?" she demanded urgently.

"She's badly bruised, and I suspect there's a sprain of the left shoulder, but no permanent damage. She needs to be kept warm and to get plenty of rest for the next few days. She's going to be fine." He observed the strained, pale face of the woman before him and added, "You could use a hot bath and some rest yourself, Ms. Yardley."

"Yes, of course," Graham replied absently, her mind occupied only with her concern for Anna. She turned to push open Anna's door and found Helen's restraining hand on her arm.

"What is it?" she asked in exasperation. All she wanted was to be alone with Anna. She must see for herself that she was safe.

"You're soaked through and shaking. You need a hot bath and you're not going in there until you have one." Helen steeled herself for what she knew was coming. As expected, Graham's well-known temper ignited.

"Please step aside, Helen," Graham ordered, reaching toward the door. "I intend to see her, and I intend to see her *now.*"

Very quietly, Helen responded, "Sweetheart, your face and hands are scratched and bleeding. You're going to scare her to death if you don't get cleaned up. Do you want her worrying about you when she should be resting?"

Graham paused, wanting to argue but knowing Helen was right. "All right, a quick one," she relented. "Please tell her I won't be long."

It was in fact only a few moments before she approached Anna's door once again, and smelled the aroma of hot tea. She followed the scent into Anna's room. Helen efficiently set up a tray and pulled a chair close to the bedside, carefully directing Graham to it.

"Now, both of you drink some of this tea," she instructed. "There's biscuits there as well." She poured two cups, guiding Graham's hand to them, and turned to leave. Anna's face was white, but the eyes she fixed on Graham's face appeared free of pain. Neither woman noticed as Helen pulled the door gently closed behind her.

"Anna?" Graham asked tentatively, leaning forward on the edge of the bed, "Are you all right?"

"I'm much better now," Anna answered softly. Graham had a welt under her right eye and a scrape on her chin where a tree limb had struck her. Even worse were the many little cuts on her hands. Thank God none of them appeared serious. "You really shouldn't be doing that sort of thing with your hands, you know. They're too precious."

"Yes, well so are you," Graham replied in a moment of unguarded honesty. She was still shaken from the accident, and not being able to see Anna, to assure herself she was truly all right, was driving her mad. She attempted to rein in her emotions, teasing lightly, "I promise I won't do it again if you promise to stay away from falling trees."

"On my honor," Anna whispered. Graham's tenderness after their weeks of estrangement, combined with the memory of her kiss moments before, had her emotions in turmoil. She needed Graham's comfort more than anything else, and here she was, gentle and attentive.

"You should rest now," Graham murmured. She edged closer to the side of the bed, carefully finding Anna's hand with her own. She traced the fragile network of veins with her sensitive fingertips, allowing her hands to trail slowly up Anna's bare arms. She fought with the urge to pull Anna into her arms, wanting desperately to shield her from harm.

Anna lay transfixed, scarcely able to breathe. She had the feeling that Graham was not aware of her actions, and that as soon as Graham realized what she was doing, she would stop. Anna fervently did not want her to stop. The possessive look on Graham's face combined with the touch of her hands was melting her with longing. The heat rising in her body overpowered the pain of her bruises. Even naked, the light sheet covering her suddenly seemed too hot to tolerate.

"I have some pills for the pain," Graham said at length. She held Anna's hand against her cheek, her fingers folded about Anna's. Very slowly, she brushed the backs of Anna's fingers against her skin. The faint touch was a balm to her anguished heart.

"I don't need them," Anna whispered, her throat tight with desire.

Graham brought one hand to Anna's face and slowly ran a few strands of her hair through her fingers. It was so soft, silken—mesmerizing in its simple beauty. She wanted nothing more than to sit there, knowing that Anna was safe beside her.

"You should sleep. I'll be here," she murmured.

Anna drew a shuddering breath. For the first time she understood the full impact of Graham's attentions. Graham was so tender, and her touch so piercing. Anna knew she had never been touched like this before.

"You should go, Graham," Anna said with effort, aware finally of the deep shadows under Graham's intense dark eyes. She couldn't bear the thought of Graham leaving, but Graham had been through nearly as much as she. The hand that held hers trembled. "You look exhausted."

"Not yet," Graham said in a tone that broached no argument.

"Then at least lie down with me," Anna demanded boldly, "or I won't sleep either."

Graham frowned. "You are rather pig-headed yourself," she remarked darkly. No one had ever been able to sway her the way Anna seemed able to. Not even Christine with all her wiles had been as hard to resist.

"I'm serious, Graham," Anna persisted, detecting a rare moment of weakness in Graham's usually impenetrable defenses. "Either you lie down with me or I'll stay awake, too."

Graham could not bring herself to leave, although she refused to consider why. With a sigh of exasperation she stretched out beside Anna, her back against the broad headboard, one arm around Anna's shoulders.

"All right now," Graham insisted, drawing Anna's head down upon her shoulder, "close your eyes."

Almost instinctively, Anna moved so that she was reclining in Graham's arms, her cheek against Graham's chest. She wrapped her uninjured arm around Graham's waist and closed her eyes. To her amazement, she soon began to drift.

"Don't leave," she murmured groggily. If she hadn't been compromised by physical and emotional stress, she never would have asked.

"I won't," Graham promised, kissing the top of her head. If she hadn't been so recently terrified for Anna's life, she never would have stayed.

When Anna opened her eyes again, it was late in the night. The tea tray had been removed, the lights turned down to a dim flicker, and the drapes drawn.

Helen, she thought, not the least concerned that the housekeeper had undoubtedly seen them lying together. At that moment it seemed the most natural thing in the world. Graham was still beside her, her cheek resting against Anna's hair, one hand rhythmically stroking the bare skin of her shoulder. In her sleep Anna had thrown her leg over Graham's thigh, and she lay tightly pressed to her now. She shifted beneath the light sheet so her breasts rested fully against Graham's chest and was rewarded with a swift gasp from Graham. Anna knew she was wet, and wondered if Graham could feel it.

"Graham," she whispered, raising herself until their lips were nearly touching. She could feel the heat radiate from Graham now, too. Graham was scarcely breathing, straining for control. Anna shifted deliberately until she lay upon Graham's body. Her nipples tensed, and she rubbed them slowly back and forth across Graham's chest. When Anna rocked against Graham's leg, a fine shudder passed through Graham's form. Relentless now with need, Anna slipped one hand along the front of Graham's trousers, trailing her fingers down Graham's thigh.

"Make love to me," Anna whispered in a voice husky with desire. "Please, Graham, please—I need you so much."

"I can't," Graham choked, shaking with the effort to contain her arousal. Her head was pounding, and each breath was an effort. Her hands clenched in the fine folds of the coverlet as she struggled not to caress the welcoming curves of Anna's body.

Anna's hand pressed into Graham's thigh, sliding higher with deliberate strokes.

"Oh God, Anna—don't," Graham groaned, her hips rising to Anna's touch of their own volition. She was losing focus, the aching in her pelvis traveling in waves into her belly and beyond. "You can't know what you're asking."

Anna saw undeniable hunger in Graham's face and a flicker of desperate need each time she stroked her. Graham was wet where she cupped her, and despite Graham's fear and resistance, Anna would not relent. She was too far gone to care, completely at the mercy of her own driving need, motivated by an instinct as essential as that to breathe.

"I *do* know what I'm asking," she gasped, "and so do you. Do you want me to beg?"

Graham hesitated still, ready to explode, trying to ignore the intolerable pressure to move against Anna's hand. Her body was in mutiny. She was afraid she might come at the slightest touch.

"Anna, you're hurt," she protested weakly.

"All I can feel is how much I need you to touch me. I'm ready. I'm so swollen—oh, God, Graham—" Anna groaned through a haze of overwhelming need, her body surging against the reed slender woman in her arms. She caught Graham's hand and brought it to the aching fullness of her breast. "Please—"

With that touch Graham's restraint finally broke. She yielded to a tidal wave of lust with a strangled cry. Her hands were upon Anna with a force that tore the breath from Anna's body.

Sweeping like wildfire down the planes of Anna's abdomen, along her thighs, ascending just as quickly to stroke her neck and breasts, Graham's touch stirred a searing heat that set Anna's nerve ends burning. She felt herself dissolving into molten liquid, her speech reduced to small cries that became incoherent whimpers as her body arched to Graham, desperately offering all of herself.

Graham's lips were on her neck, murmuring her name like a benediction. She eased her body over Anna's, brushing the covers aside, one hand seeking between Anna's legs. She thrilled to the welcoming warmth, parting the engorged lips, groaning as she slipped into Anna's silken depths. She clenched her jaw, willing herself to go slowly, struggling with the shattering urge to claim Anna with all the power of her passion.

"Oh God, Graham," Anna cried out as Graham filled her, willing her deeper, thrusting to contain all of her. Graham's mouth bruised her lips, the fabric of Graham's shirt chaffed her swollen nipples, and the exquisite motion of Graham's fingers within her inflamed her senses.

"Oh, no," she gasped urgently as her hips began to rock involuntarily. Her clitoris was tingling, jumping with the rhythm of Graham's thrusting fingers. *Oh God—not so soon.* "Graham wait."

But it was already too late. Muscles clenched and tightening painfully, she sobbed as her body, long denied, hurtled toward release. She clutched Graham's shoulders, strangling on her own throaty cries. Endlessly, she peaked, only to be driven to a higher plateau by the insistent stroking of Graham's finely tuned hands, until she lay exhausted, able only to murmur, "Enough, my darling, I'll die from you."

Graham laughed gently, her fingers quieting, but not withdrawing. She settled Anna firmly against her, breathing into her hair, "Oh no, love, you won't die from this. Never from this."

Through a curtain of languorous fatigue, Anna saw Graham's dark eyes upon her face, tender and deep with passion. To see her so stopped the breath in her throat, she loved her so much. Anna pressed closer to her, whispering, "Just hold me, please."

"Anything," Graham murmured as Anna drifted into sleep.

Anna awakened slowly, her body still pulsing with sensation. Graham still held her tightly. She lay with her eyes closed, savoring the sweet satisfaction of Graham's nearness and the lingering aftermath of their lovemaking. She didn't move when she felt a featherlight touch upon her cheek, remaining silent as Graham's fingers traced her face. As gently as butterflies on spring blossoms, Graham stroked her brows, each eyelid, and the line of her lips and nose. With both hands she cupped Anna's face, her thumbs brushing across the bones of her cheeks to sweep along her jaw and chin. A fingertip pressed against the pulse beating in her neck, then moved to circle the curve of her ear. When at last the gently probing hands quieted on her skin, Anna questioned softly, "Can you see me?"

Graham smiled faintly. "Yes."

"You make me feel beautiful," Anna confessed shyly.

"You *are* beautiful, Anna." Graham kissed her softly, reverently.

Anna smiled, then stretched indolently, trying to dispel the intoxicating lethargy Graham's touch induced. She shifted on the bed, one hand resting on Graham's abdomen. Muscles fluttered beneath her fingers. Being this close to Graham kept her constantly aroused. It was a new experience, one that left her breathless.

Graham, ever sensitive, raised one questioning eyebrow. "What is it?"

"I want to look at you—all of you," Anna replied, tugging at Graham's shirt, brushing her fingers along the taut muscles beneath. She slipped her hand beneath the waistband of the tailored linen trousers, her pulse racing as Graham groaned and shuddered faintly at the touch.

"Let me touch you," Anna whispered against Graham's neck. She wanted her, as much as she had wanted Graham to take her just a short time ago.

Graham flushed, but sat up slightly and began to unbutton her shirt. She shrugged the soft material from her shoulders and reached for the zipper on her trousers.

Anna stilled Graham's hand, whispering, "Let me."

Graham raised her hips as Anna slid the last of her clothing away.

"God, you're perfect," Anna breathed, gazing at the sweeping planes of Graham's long form. As slowly as she knew how, Anna began to touch her, lingering over each curve and hollow, exploring her with her hands and lips. She wanted to make the moment last forever, and even as Graham's breathing quickened, her body undulating under Anna's caresses, Anna went slowly. With her mouth she began a slow descent from Graham's neck, teasing each nipple before she traced a path down Graham's quivering abdomen.

Graham opened before her, arching gently up to meet Anna's tongue, her breath rasping in her throat. As Anna's lips drew on her engorged clitoris, she moaned softly, her fingers entwining in Anna's hair. Silently, her hands guided Anna to her.

Anna had never known such tender power before. She thrilled to her ability to please this woman who had given her such exquisite pleasure. Her tongue stroked each ripe fold, moving with the surges of Graham's body, matching her rhythm to that of her beloved. She was drunk with the taste of her, drowning in her rich nectar.

Graham groaned, grasped Anna's hands tightly, and arched against her lips. "Ah, Anna—my love," she whispered brokenly, finally giving in to the relentless driving pressure to come.

Anna struggled to hear Graham's cries through the deafening roar of her own raging lust. She moaned with each quake that rippled through Graham's body, holding fast to the slender hips until Graham quieted. Were it not for Graham calling her name, she would have gladly stayed there, senses overflowing, for time out of mind. Eventually Graham's hands drew her gently upwards, bringing her back to awareness.

"Come here," Graham whispered. "I need you close to me."

Anna moved to lie beside her, her heart contracting at the sight of tears streaking Graham's cheeks. She thought she might come apart. She wanted so much to ease the pain Graham had suffered for so long. Softly she brushed the tears away. Her lips caressed the scar on Graham's brow, lingering over each translucent eyelid. Graham's lips parted in silent pleasure and a long sigh escaped her.

"You make me feel more than I ever imagined possible," Anna murmured against the ivory column of Graham's neck. "It's almost more than my heart can contain."

Graham caressed her gently as Anna slipped once more into satisfied sleep. Graham lay quietly for a long time, trying to absorb every sensation, every sound, every scent that was Anna. She filled her heart, and her mind, and her memory with her. At last she slipped from the bed, leaning down to softly kiss the sleeping woman.

"You are more beautiful than any music I have ever heard," she whispered.

The sun rose over Yardley's grand expanses, but the brilliance of the changing dawn colors was lost on the woman who stood high above the sea. The brisk ocean breeze tossed her hair into her eyes, but she did not lift a hand to shield them. The tears on her face were not from the wind, nor the shivering in her body from the piercing cold. In the long years of her exile, she had never been so alone. Her defenses had been breached, her heart rent by the gentle touch of a woman's lips. She remembered with shattering clarity each sensation—the longing and the wonder and the miracle of communion, body and soul. She could not drive the memory of the past from her thoughts—the complete desolation of the spirit she had suffered when Christine left her. She feared that ultimately her deepest needs would force Anna to leave her, too. She knew with utter certainty that this would be a pain she could not bear a second time in her life. Despite the years, the wounds still bled, and she could not banish the fear. She had not sought this love; in fact she had hidden herself from the very possibility of it for years. She cried for what she had done, and what she must do. Finally, she returned to the house to await Anna's awakening, and to seal her own fate.

Anna knew instinctively as she reached out that she was alone. "Graham?" she called.

"I'm here, Anna," Graham answered from her place by the window. "How do you feel?

Anna rolled over and pushed herself up in bed. She regarded Graham carefully. She had grown too used to the nuances of Graham's posture and tone of voice not to know when she was distressed. "I'm stiff, and sore just about everywhere, but nothing feels seriously damaged," she replied cautiously.

"Good," Graham sighed. She gathered herself for the hardest words she would ever say. "Anna, I must talk to you about last night."

Anna closed her eyes, her stomach tightening. Last night she didn't need to think. All she knew was the joy of Graham's presence. She didn't need to think *now* to know she had been more deeply moved by Graham's touch than any other event in her life. She didn't need words to capture the ecstasy of loving this woman. Her skin still tingled from the stroke of Graham's hands, her body stirred with desire at the mere sight of her. She loved her, more passionately than she would have believed possible. Graham Yardley had claimed her, willingly or not—heart, body and soul.

"You don't need to say anything, Graham," Anna replied. "Last night, with you, was more beautiful than anything I've ever experienced. No one has ever touched me—"

Graham interrupted her harshly. She could not bear to hear these words. "Anna, you were hurt, vulnerable—you needed comforting. I—I was frightened for you. I forgot myself. It wasn't meant. I'm sorry."

"What are you saying? Are you trying to tell me last night was some kind of *mistake*?" Anna asked incredulously. She stared at Graham uncomprehendingly. "You can't mean that. For God's sake, Graham—"

"We were both frightened, exhausted—I took advantage," Graham stated flatly.

"Graham! *I* asked you into my bed. I've been wanting, needing you, for so long. God Graham! I *love* you," Anna cried vehemently.

Graham groaned. "Anna, Anna, you must not." She drew a deep breath, her face set. "Last night should never have happened. I have no desire for it to be repeated. I do not want that kind of relationship with you."

"And you expect me to simply forget it? What we shared—the way it felt to touch you?" Anna questioned grimly, her hurt and bewilderment giving way to anger. "And what am I supposed to do with my feelings for you, Graham? Am I to ignore them the way you seem to be able to? "

Graham gave no sign that Anna's words affected her at all. "There can be no question of anything other than a friendship between us. If I've misled you, I apologize."

Anna wanted to scream; part of her wanted to beg. How could she be alone in this? She had felt love in Graham's touch. She had heard it as Graham whispered her name. She stared at Graham, a cold hand gripping her heart. "Are you sure?" she asked at last.

"I'm quite sure." Her face betrayed not a flicker of emotion.

"Then I'll be leaving Yardley as soon as I can make arrangements," Anna replied hollowly, her mind numb with pain.

Graham clenched her hands, steeling herself against the crushing desolation. "Of course, if you think you must."

Anna watched her cross to the door, knowing this might be the last time she saw her. As Graham's hand touched the knob, Anna said coldly, "Damn you for a coward, Graham Yardley. How can you do this?"

Graham faltered for a second before wordlessly closing the door gently behind her.

"At least tell me what she's done," Helen cried frantically as she watched Anna pile boxes into the back of her Jeep.

"She hasn't *done* anything," Anna replied woodenly. "She's exactly the same as she's always been. I was the one who made the mistake."

"Let me talk to her," Helen pleaded. "Just tell me what happened."

Anna stifled a laugh that verged on tears. She felt dangerously out of control. *Poor Helen, this is almost as hard on her as it is on me. The only one who seems unaffected by all this is Graham.*

"There's nothing you can do, Helen," she responded when she could find her voice.

Helen stopped her hurried motions with a hand on her arm, forcing Anna to look at her. "Anna," she said quietly, "it will kill her if you leave."

"No, Helen," Anna said as she gently removed her hand and stepped up into the Jeep. "It will kill me."

She did not look back as she drove away from all she loved.

CHAPTER SEVENTEEN

Anna woke before the alarm after another restless night. She turned toward the window, seeking a hint of the sun through the glass. Even after all this time she still missed the smell of the ocean. She lay quietly, waiting for the ache in her to lessen. It was there each day when she opened her eyes, arising from some deep wound that would not heal. Pain was her constant companion, a raw burning grief that clouded even the simplest pleasures. She had learned to accept it, as she accepted that there was a place in her soul that would remain forever empty. That she loved Graham still, would always love her, was the truth and the agony she lived with.

After the first desolate weeks alone again in Boston, she tried to reclaim her life. She immersed herself in her studies and had only to complete her thesis to have her degree. She had no social life and desired none. There was no question of re-entering the world she had known during her marriage—a world now foreign to her. Loving Graham had taught her that she could only have loved with such deep passion and paralyzing desire because Graham was a woman. And she knew without doubt that no other woman could ever eclipse Graham in her heart.

She wanted Graham still with a ferocity that stunned her. She need only to recall some fleeting image, and she would be ambushed by desire—her need to touch her, to taste her, to lose herself in her was palpable. Anna welcomed these moments, despite the bitter pain of loss, because it was only their presence that convinced her some part of her still lived. Otherwise, she moved through her days numb and scarcely present. The future stretched before her with no hint of joy.

The alarm sounded, a reminder that each day would come, and that she would somehow survive. As she moved about her small studio apartment gathering her things, she tried to dispel the lingering memories of her past. Woven through the tapestry of loss was a hard bitter thread of anger, anger over the life, and the love, she might have had—things too painful to dwell on now.

She still found it hard to believe the direction her life had taken. She now worked for a landscape design firm, a job that a year ago she would have been overjoyed to have. She did enjoy her work, in fact, it was her salvation, but the pleasure was diminished by the emptiness of the rest of her life. She barely remembered how she had gotten through that initial interview.

Lauren Parker, a nationally renowned landscape architect and one of a very few women to head her own firm, had interviewed her personally. Anna recalled that Lauren had been both direct and personable, questioning Anna thoroughly but in an easy relaxed manner. Apparently she had been impressed by Anna's graduate work on historic estate renovations, an area she said her firm was interested in exploring. Although it seemed now to Anna that she had stumbled through the interview in a daze, she must have made a favorable impression. She had been there six months. She grabbed her briefcase and hurried toward the door. She needed this job, but more importantly, she needed to work. It was the only thing that provided brief respite from her memories.

Anna was sketching in the details of an outdoor theatre when someone tapped on the wall of her work cubicle. She looked up to find Lauren leaning against the partition. It wasn't unusual for Lauren Parker to supervise the work of her staff personally, but she managed to do it in a way that was both non-threatening and non-intrusive. Those who worked for her knew how fortunate they were to have an employer who was talented as well as fair-minded. Anna smiled a greeting, laying her work aside. "Hi."

"Hi. How's the prospectus for the Randolph estate?" Lauren was dressed casually in a navy linen pants suit that accentuated her trim athletic build. She could have been thirty-five, although Anna knew she was at least ten years older. She radiated confidence and vigorous good health. Her blonde hair was stylishly short, and she wore almost no makeup.

"Good, I think. I have some things to run by Don, and then it should be ready for you to look at."

Lauren nodded. "Excellent. We're ahead of schedule, which should appease those elements on Randolph's board of directors who thought the project should go to Tom Langdon across town." Despite her firm's national reputation, there were always those who mistrusted the ability of a woman to excel in a man's field. This job was her entree into the realm of historic renovation she had been waiting for.

Lauren hesitated a second, then asked, "How about a working dinner tonight? I'd like to hear what you've come up with so far, but I've got clients scheduled all afternoon. If you don't have other plans? I know it's Friday night."

A shadow flickered across Anna's face and was quickly gone. "No," she said quietly, "I don't have any plans. Dinner would be fine. Should I meet you somewhere?"

"Why don't we just grab a cab from here?" Lauren hadn't missed the reaction her invitation had provoked. Whatever the memory, it had hurt. She said nothing further, knowing Anna was intensely private.

Anna nodded, "Okay."

Lauren smiled warmly. "Good. I'm looking forward to it."

At six o'clock Lauren stopped in the corridor beside Anna's desk. "Are you ready to finish up? The cab should be downstairs in about fifteen minutes."

Anna smiled up at her, nodding. "I'm more than ready. I'll just freshen up and meet you outside."

Lauren held the cab door open while Anna slid in, then instructed the driver, "The Copley Plaza, please," as she settled next to Anna with a sigh. "God, I've been looking forward to this all day."

"I might be a little under-dressed for the Copley," Anna said, indicating her casual slacks and sweater.

Lauren turned her head to look at Anna. "Nonsense. You look terrific," she said softly. The woman beside her had lost the deep tan that had accentuated her blue eyes and blond hair so strikingly six months before, but she had also lost the haunted look that seemed to shadow her every moment. She smiled occasionally now, a blazing smile that never failed to capture Lauren's attention for just long enough to be distracting. Pleasantly distracting.

Anna blushed under Lauren's warm, appraising glance. It was nothing like the way men had looked at her, still did in fact. She didn't feel as if she were being assessed like a painting about to be purchased, or a fine wine about to be consumed. Lauren's glance was appreciative, and intimate in a respectful way. It was the first time Anna had ever been aware of a woman looking at her in quite that manner. Would Graham have, if she could have seen her? Without warning she remembered the way Graham had stroked her face after they made love, 'seeing' her in the only way she could. Anna recognized the sensuality of Lauren's gaze because she had felt it, magnified a thousand times, in Graham's hands on her skin. The image was so painful she closed her eyes with a small gasp.

"What is it?" Lauren asked in concern.

"Just a headache," Anna said with a shaky laugh. "I think I forgot lunch and it's catching up with me."

"Well, dinner is on the company," Lauren said, almost as if she didn't own it. "Let's enjoy it." She doubted the headache story; she had seen the same thing happen to Anna before. Some word or gesture would inexplicably cause her to pale, visibly shaken. Something had hurt her badly, and Lauren guessed that Anna kept the anguish at bay through sheer strength of will. Anna's struggle touched some deep cord in Lauren, as she watched the younger woman slowly rise above her pain over the past months. "Come on," she said, touching Anna's hand briefly. "Let me buy you a drink."

Anna forced herself to relax, wanting to forget everything for just a little while. She decided to try to enjoy herself, and before she knew it, she was seated with Lauren at a cozy table sipping a very fine wine.

At Lauren's suggestion, they got business out of the way while they waited for appetizers, so that by the time their meal came, their conversation was casual. Anna found Lauren an easy companion. Her interests beyond the professional were varied, and she had a way of bringing images to life with her enthusiasm. She was bright, gracious and altogether charming. For the first time in months Anna found she could actually distance herself from the despair that seemed to be the undercurrent of her life. She was grateful for the brief surcease of pain.

"Anna," Lauren said as she reached to fill Anna's wine glass, "you have been doing excellent work at the firm, and I consider us lucky to have you. I hope you plan to stay on with us for the long term. There will be plenty of opportunity for advancement."

Anna stared at her in surprise. She hadn't expected Lauren to notice her work, let alone comment so favorably upon it. She was pleased and said so.

Lauren nodded, her face uncharacteristically subdued. She fidgeted briefly with her straw, then tossed it onto the table with a sigh. "There's never an easy way to do this, at least none that I've ever found," she said at length. "But I want you to understand that this has absolutely nothing to do with work, and never will. No matter what you say to me, your position at the firm is based upon your production, and your skill—nothing else."

Anna looked at her quizzically. "I don't have the faintest idea what you're talking about," she said.

Lauren blushed and laughed lightly. "How could you? I'm not saying anything." She leaned forward slightly, her intense gray eyes fixed on Anna's. "Anna—I think you are a very attractive woman, and I like you. I would very much like to spend more time with you—socially. Well, romantically actually."

Anna stared at her, at a loss for words. Lauren was highly attractive in many ways—bright, accomplished, physically compelling, and Anna was more comfortable with her than she had been in months. Part of her wanted this woman to make her forget Graham Yardley.

Lauren waited in silence, then asked softly, "Have I misread you? If I have, I apologize."

Anna cleared her throat, then responded, "No, you haven't—I mean, I am a lesbian."

Lauren added in concern, "I have never asked an employee out before. I meant it, Anna—don't think for a second that this has any bearing on your position at the firm. Please."

Anna searched for her voice. "I don't—it doesn't feel that way, and neither do you."

She looked at the woman across from her, imagining her touch, her kiss. She had grown to admire and respect Lauren, and after tonight she knew she liked her. She wondered if she could let Lauren make love to her, if the physical sensation might even be welcome, if it might somehow dull her memory of Graham even briefly. She longed for some relief from the endless torment, but she knew without a shred of doubt she could never give Lauren her heart. That was no longer hers to own, or to give. She was Graham's, in every fiber of her being, and always would be. She looked at Lauren helplessly, "It's not that—it's just—oh, God. I can't, Lauren, I'm sorry—"

Lauren thought she detected tears in her eyes. "Hey," she said softly, "it's okay. I didn't mean to upset you."

Anna shook her head, brushing impatiently at the moisture on her cheeks. "You haven't. This has been the best night I've spent in months. And if things were different—"

Lauren hurried to state, "I don't want to get in the middle of anything if you're already involved with someone. I've never heard you mention anyone."

"No," Anna answered, the pain in her voice impossible to hide. "I'm not involved with anyone."

"But?" Lauren questioned gently.

Anna's gaze was wounded. "But there is someone I love, very much. Someone who apparently doesn't love me. But that doesn't stop the wanting, does it?"

Lauren looked at her sympathetically. "No, it doesn't. Perhaps time will help. I've enjoyed our evening together. And I'd like to do it again sometime. I appreciate your honesty, Anna, and if the time comes that you might feel differently about seeing me, I'll consider myself lucky. 'Til then—friends?"

Anna smiled tremulously. "I could use a friend. Thank you, Lauren."

CHAPTER EIGHTEEN

As time passed Lauren proved true to her word. On the average of once a week, she invited Anna to the theatre or out for dinner. The only place Anna refused to accompany her was to the symphony. In Anna's mind, the concert stage would always belong to Graham, and the thought of being in a concert hall where every sight and sound would remind her of Graham brought twisting pain to her depths. Seeing Anna's response the first time she asked her, Lauren never asked her again.

Anna enjoyed their time together, coming to value their relationship immensely. She would not speak of her past, and Lauren did not press her. When they parted, Lauren kissed her lightly on the cheek. It didn't escape Anna's notice that occasionally Lauren would look at her with a question in her eyes, but Anna never felt pressured to move their relationship onto a more intimate level. Anna hoped that their friendship was as rewarding to Lauren as it had come to be to her. Early one morning the phone on her desk rang. It was Lauren.

"Can I see you in my office for a minute?"

"I'll be right there," Anna replied, rolling up the plan she had been working on.

When Anna entered, Lauren motioned for Anna to join her at the large drafting table situated before the enormous windows overlooking the Boston Commons. She indicated a layout pinned to the board. She was clearly excited.

"The Randolph renovations have progressed exceptionally well. The article featuring our work in the Times last weekend has really fostered interest in estate reclamation. This area is ripe for it. I think it's time to push the promotional we discussed when you first interviewed. I'd like to use your work at Yardley as the centerpiece. It's one of the oldest estates on the Cape and will be easily recognized by prospective clients. Since Yardley is so well known to you, and the concept of marketing estate landscape restoration is really yours as well, I'd like you to oversee the project. We'll need detailed plans, as well as photo documentation. I want you to put your other projects on hold until this is off the ground."

Anna stood stunned and speechless, while Lauren looked at her expectantly. Of course she should be honored that Lauren would entrust such an important project to her direction, and it was what she had been training to do—but, oh God, not at Yardley. Her composure threatened to give way under a wave of panic.

"I can't," she finally whispered.

Lauren stared at her in astonishment. "What do you mean, 'you can't?' Is it because of your thesis? I thought you had that nearly wrapped up."

"No," Anna forced herself to say calmly. "I'll work on the promotional—anything else you want. Anything. But I can't do the work on Yardley."

"But Anna, I want Yardley as the main work. That's where I need you."

Anna passed a trembling hand across her face, trying to gather her wits. Just the mention of Yardley had brought a flood of memories, and such pain she thought she might be ill. God, what would she do if she actually had to see Graham? It was impossible. She couldn't do it.

"Anna, we're friends. Tell me what this is all about." Lauren laid her hand gently on Anna's arm, her concern genuine. Anna was trembling.

Anna turned to face her, an agony of despair clearly visible. Lauren had never seen such desolation, and her heart surged with compassion.

"Tell me, sweetheart."

"I can't go back to Yardley," Anna said at last, her voice shaking. "Why not?"

"Graham," Anna began, barely able to say her name. "I can't see her. I can't." She looked at Lauren pleadingly. "Please don't ask me to, Lauren. It would kill me."

Lauren studied her for long moments, the pieces slowly falling into place. She knew that Anna had lived at Yardley but had never given it any thought. Now Anna's isolation and depression were more understandable.

"Graham Yardley—the composer," Lauren said softly. "She's the woman you're in love with, isn't she?"

Anna closed her eyes, trying to stem the tears, failing. "Yes," she choked out, turning from her friend, struggling for control. She felt a tender hand on her shoulder, heard a soft voice murmur her name, and she turned into the arms that waited for her. Lauren held her gently, letting her cry, not trying to tell her it was all right when it so obviously wasn't. At length Anna drew away, fumbling for a tissue, embarrassed.

"I'm sorry," she said. "I didn't expect this. If I don't think about her, I seem to be able to manage. You took me by surprise."

Lauren let out a long breath. "Anna, you've always been honest with me and I care about you. I don't want to see you suffer like this any longer, and I'll admit not all of my reasons are selfless ones. I won't pretend that I don't want more from our relationship, but this isn't about that. This is destroying you. You need to give her up. You have the rest of your life, don't allow it to be an empty one. Maybe if you work on the project, it will help you heal."

Anna laughed almost hysterically. "Heal? You can't heal what's already dead, and that's what I am, Lauren. Dead inside. All I'm trying to do now is make it from day to day. If I have to see Graham, I won't even be able to do that. She's not something I can just 'give up'. She's in every part of me. You can't imagine what being near her is like for me."

Lauren winced at the truth of Anna's words. It wasn't easy to be faced with the extent of Anna's passion for another woman, but nevertheless her tone was kind as she offered, "You won't have to see her. She isn't there."

Anna grasped the edge of the table, her head suddenly light. "Oh, dear God, has something happened to her? Is she all right?"

"As far as I know, she is. David Norcross told me that no one had been in residence at Yardley since last fall, but that he would provide us with keys if we needed access." Seeing the look of panic on Anna's face, she added gently, "That's really all I know."

Anna forced down the surge of panic. "I can't make a decision about this now, Lauren. Give me a little time—just a few days, please."

Lauren nodded, reluctantly accepting that Anna's heart still belonged completely to Graham Yardley. Despite her own disappointment, as a friend, she would have to let Anna find her own way. "I'll need your answer by the end of next week," she conceded.

That night Anna dreamed of Yardley, and of Graham. A storm was coming, like the storm that brought down the sycamore. She was in the garden, the sky darkening around her. Turning to the sea, she saw Graham standing at the edge of the cliff, struggling to stay upright in the gale. She seemed even thinner in the distant gloom, wraithlike, and in danger of being swept from the earth by the force of the snarling winds. Anna's cries to her were flung back in her face by the howling blasts. She must reach her.

"Graham, I'm coming," she screamed soundlessly, "I'm coming, my darling!" She fought to move, choking with panic, able only to watch in horror as Graham was flung by the whirlwind into the raging waters.

"No!" she wailed into the night, finally dragging herself to consciousness. She lay gasping, soaked in sweat, her face streaked with tears. The aftermath of her dream left her awash with loss. "Oh God, Graham," she whispered into the darkness, "I love you so much."

Anna drove slowly up the drive to Yardley Manor, her heart pounding. Yardley appeared abandoned, dark and foreboding. The shutters were all closed, and windswept debris littered the walks and the wide front porch. She parked her Jeep behind the house by the kitchen and walked down the steep garden path toward the sea. She stopped at the site of the fallen sycamore, thinking of how that accident had finally brought Graham into her arms. Oh God, she thought she had found heaven. How could she have been so wrong? She stood for many minutes looking out to the sea, images flashing through her mind like slides on a screen. She recalled how Graham had looked that first day in the library, pale and stern, and so stubborn and proud. She had been drawn to her even then. She remembered the slow building of her love as she had come to know more of the gentle, tortured soul Graham kept hidden within. What finally started tears flowing was the memory of Graham's music—its haunting beauty and the even more beautiful image of Graham playing. As the music cascaded through her mind, so too did the remembrance of their lovemaking. She ached for Graham's touch, and to touch her in return.

Watching the waves crash below, ominous in their fury, she was reminded of the desolation she had felt in her dream. She couldn't continue to live like this. Anna felt a strange steeling of her heart, and a new determination. Replacing the pain that accompanied each breath was a rising anger, and the resolution to put an end to this torment. As she turned and began the long climb back, Anna became aware of another sensation in her heart. She finally recognized that it was hope.

CHAPTER NINETEEN

I'm afraid I simply cannot reveal that information. I'm truly sorry."

Anna looked at David Norcross and repeated determinedly, "I must see her. Where has she gone?"

Norcross sighed. "I have strict instructions that no one is to be given that information. If you'd like, you can leave a message." His look suggested there was little chance that Graham would return anyone's message.

Anna shook her head. "No, I need to talk to her in person."

"If it were a matter of life or death, perhaps."

"Mr. Norcross, it *is* a matter of life or death. My life and hers." Seeing the surprised look on his face, Anna continued, her eyes locked on his. "I love Graham Yardley. And she loves me—I hope. I let her drive me away, but I can't believe that's what she really wants. Please, I must see her. Now, before it's too late." Even as she spoke, she struggled with a strange sense of foreboding. She couldn't dispel the feeling that something was terribly wrong.

David Norcross pushed his chair back and went to stand at the windows that rose above Boston Harbor. As his silence grew, Anna remained still, scarcely daring to breathe.

When he spoke at last, it was as if to himself. "I have known Graham Yardley since she was a young girl. Her father was one of my closest friends. Graham's accident nearly killed him, but you must know that," he said, turning to look fully at Anna. "Graham survived, but something vital was lost—her joy, her incredible passion, her great talent—all gone. We all lost something as a result, and the world lost a great artist."

Anna nodded. "I know that, but it doesn't have to be that way. It's still part of her, Mr. Norcross—undiminished. She's been hurt, and she's afraid. *I* was afraid, and I failed us both. Please help us."

Norcross bent over his desk, wrote quickly on a piece of stationery and handed the slip of paper across the desk to Anna.

"I wish you luck, my dear. For all of our sakes."

"Oh my Lord, is it really you?"

Anna swept Helen up into her arms, hugging her fiercely.

"Yes, Helen, it's really me." She stepped back to gaze at the older woman, instantly struck by the signs of distress and worry in her face. For the first time since Anna had known her, she looked every one of her sixty-three years. Something was wrong. "Is she here, Helen?"

Helen nodded. "She's out in the gazebo." Helen's voice caught on a sob, and she turned away to hide her tears. "I was just taking her tea. I'll ask her if she'll see you."

Anna gently restrained the older woman with a hand on her arm. "No you won't. This time it isn't up to her. I intend to talk to her."

"Then you'd better prepare yourself. She's ill."

Something in the way Helen looked told more than her words. Icy fear gripped Anna's heart. "Tell me."

Helen's voice trembled as she recounted the events of the last few terrifying weeks. "She came down with pneumonia—six weeks ago, I think. For some reason the doctors couldn't explain to me, she didn't respond the way they expected to the medicines. They said there was something wrong with her resistance, but—"

"What do you think?" Anna asked, her throat painfully tight.

Helen looked at Anna sadly, then replied, "I think she didn't care if she got well. I've seen Graham through what I thought were the worst times of her life, and I've never seen her like this."

"Why are you here? Why did you leave Yardley?" Anna asked, fighting her panic, struggling to understand what was happening.

Helen tried not to sound harsh, but her fear outweighed her concern for Anna's feelings. "I told you what would happen if you left her. She wouldn't stay there a day after you moved out. Ordered a car, told me to close the house, and left for Philadelphia that night. She's been alone with her piano day and night, worse than I've ever seen her. One final work, she said, and she's been at it frantically for months. No wonder the doctors couldn't help. I know what's she's doing. When this is done, she means to leave us." Helen broke into quiet sobs.

"Oh Jesus," Anna whispered, her eyes closed tightly against the thought. "Why didn't you call me? You must have known I would come."

"I almost did, especially those few days when she was so ill. It looked like we might lose her—"

"Oh, God," Anna groaned. *Please don't let this be happening.*

"But she made me promise that I wouldn't. She didn't want your pity, she said."

"My God, she's a fool—but no more so than I," Anna said harshly. "I called her a coward, but I'm the one who was the coward. I knew what she had been through. I knew about Christine. Eventually she would have accepted that I loved her, if only I had stayed."

"It wasn't your love she doubted," Helen corrected gently.

"Then what?" Anna cried in frustration.

"She was afraid of her love for you—afraid it would be too much. She never believed that you would stay."

"And I left her, didn't I?" Anna said bitterly. "This is madness. I have to make her hear me, Helen. I love her so much."

"Just don't let her send you away," Helen said firmly, beginning to hope for the first time in months. "She'll try to, you know."

Anna shook her head grimly. "I won't leave if there's any part of her that loves me—no matter what she says."

Helen smiled, "Then I needn't worry. Just go to her, my dear girl."

Graham stood at the rear of the open gazebo, her back to the entrance. Anna paused at the threshold, paralyzed with the reality of seeing her again. She appeared even thinner; Anna could see that she had lost weight. Each tendon in the fine hand that rested on the rail stood out in stark contrast to the overlying skin, stretched to near translucency. Even from a distance Anna saw the tremor in the delicate fingers. She wanted so much to hold her, but she held back. They must talk.

"Thank you, Helen—just leave it, please," Graham said in a low voice. After a moment she tilted her head, listening, "Helen?"

"Hello, darling," Anna called softly, her voice catching in her throat.

Graham swayed slightly and the hand that clutched the railing turned white.

"Anna?" she whispered in disbelief. Abruptly she turned, her dark eyes searching for a figure she would never see, "Anna?"

Anna gasped and took an uncertain step forward. Graham looked so ill. Her normally brilliant gaze was clouded with pain. Her face was gaunt and lined with fatigue. But even more frightening than the dark circles smudging her normally clear skin was her obvious physical weakness. She leaned heavily on her walking stick, and without it Anna was sure she would fall.

"Yes, it's me," she said, struggling to keep the fear from showing in her voice. "I'm sorry it's taken me so long to get here."

Graham straightened with difficulty. She would not have Anna here because of her weakness. With a semblance of her previous authority she demanded, "Did Helen send for you?"

"No, darling, she didn't. I came because I couldn't bear being separated from you any longer. I've missed you so much."

"I don't want your pity, Anna," Graham snapped, her tone harsh. "And I don't want you here because of my needs." Sagging slightly despite her best efforts, she passed a trembling hand across her face. In a strained voice, she pleaded, "I have little left but my pride, Anna. Please leave me that."

Anna crossed the distance between them to grasp Graham's shoulders in her hands. "Not your needs, Graham—*mine*. I need you— more than you'll ever know. I need your strength and your passion and your desire. And, oh God, I need your music." She tightened her hold, fearing that Graham would somehow slip away. "My life is so barren without you. Please won't you let me come home?"

Graham bowed her head, eyes closed. "Anna, I don't know if I can—I don't know if I dare."

This time Anna would not be denied. She would not give up. "What can't you do, darling? Is it that you don't want me?"

Graham couldn't resist a fleeting caress against Anna's cheek. She had thought never to feel her again. She had tried so hard to deny what she knew to be true—that she loved her with the last beat of her heart. As her touch lingered, she remembered each moment of their last night together. Her breath caught painfully in her throat. Softly she said, "Yes, I want you—more than life itself."

"Then what?" Anna persisted, catching Graham's fingers, bestowing a fleeting kiss to her palm. "Tell me why you won't let me love you."

Graham drew a shuddering breath, her eyes closed against the pain. "I'm afraid that if I do, it will happen again. I am everything Christine accused me of being—possessive, demanding, consuming in my need—I'm afraid if I take you into my life, *all* of my life, I'll drive you away just as I did Christine. It would be worse than death if I lost you then, Anna."

The last words emerged as a strangled whisper, and the anguish in Graham's voice fueled Anna's anger. Christine had ruled Graham's life, even in her absence, for far too long. She would not rule her future, or Anna's.

"I am *not* Christine, Graham! I love you, and I will go on loving you whether you will have me or not. There is nothing you could do, short of not loving me, that would ever make me leave you. I am not afraid of your needs, or your wants, or your passions. I want you. I want to spend my life with you—loving you, being loved by you." She stepped closer until her body pressed lightly against Graham's, forcing her to feel her passion. "Tell me you don't love me, Graham—tell me you don't want me—and I'll go."

"I can't," Graham groaned, trembling at Anna's nearness. She hadn't been born strong enough to resist this torture.

"I have made my choice, Graham, and I choose you." Anna kissed her, a kiss too quickly ended. "You have to choose whether or not you want me. But choose for the right reasons. Choose out of love—not out of fear."

It was the kiss that undid her. It stirred every emotion she had tried to bury since the day Anna left her. She needed her, she wanted her, and she could not go on without her. She had no choice; Anna offered her life. With a moan deep in her throat, she surrendered. Her lips sought Anna's and were answered with an urgency that matched her own. They kissed fervently, their bodies fusing, swaying together as they reaffirmed their possession of one another.

Anna verged on losing control, and leaned back unsteadily, her arms locked around Graham's waist, trying to reduce the shaking of her legs. Graham gasped against her neck, groaning in protest at her withdrawal.

"I want you so much," Graham murmured, insistent, one hand sliding under the loose fabric at Anna's waist. Her hand moved lower, seeking the hot welcoming wetness.

"Graham, wait," Anna said with effort. "We can't do this here."

"I don't intend to let you go," Graham growled, her lips seeking Anna's again.

"Does this mean you love me?" Anna teased gently, pressing both hands against Graham's chest, restraining her for a moment.

"Eternally my love," Graham affirmed, pulling her close. "Eternally."

The room Graham led her to was dimly lit by a fire burning in a huge fireplace. A four-poster canopy bed faced the hearth from the opposite side of the room. Two glasses and a chilled bottle of champagne stood on the bedside table. Graham stopped inside the door, suddenly uncertain, her face questioning. Anna smiled softly as her grip on Graham's hand tightened.

"I haven't changed my mind. I'll never change my mind about loving you," Anna whispered gently. "Don't make me wait to show you how much I love you, darling. It's been far too long already."

They undressed with urgent hands, caressing each other with the wonder of newly discovered love. It was Anna who drew them to the bed, guiding Graham down, resting upon her gently. She wanted her, the want like a fierce hunger in her soul. She ached with the urgency to touch her. Her body screamed for the release only those exquisite hands could give her. She left a pool of moisture on Graham's leg where it pressed to her. Her clitoris threatened to burst from the blood coursing into it. She resisted her demanding need, aware of Graham's physical fragility. She shook with the effort it required for her to hold back.

Graham pulled her nearer with surprising strength. "I need you, Anna—now," she whispered. "It's all I need. Please."

As gently as she knew how, Anna took her. Her lips caressed the hollow of Graham's neck and the rise of her breast, pausing to suckle a nipple, explore her navel. Her hands stroked firm muscles and trembling limbs, coming to rest gently in the moist warm sanctuary between her thighs. Tenderly she parted the full, silky folds, breathing her scent, stroking the length of her, softly tonguing the quivering clitoris. She was aware only of the heat of Graham's flesh beneath her lips, and the breathtaking wonder of her cries filling the air. After the long months of waiting, Anna didn't think she could ever touch her enough. She was amazed to feel her own body climb nearer and nearer orgasm with each thrust of Graham's hips against her face, each contraction of Graham's muscles around her fingers. Anna groaned as the spasms began at the base of her clitoris and traveled down her legs, into her belly, and finally coalesced into one continuous explosion behind her tightly closed eyes. When she came, Graham murmured her name, and Anna knew a joy beyond anything she had ever dreamed. Long into the night they loved, stopping only to whisper their devotion, seeking and giving the reassurances they needed to heal.

As morning broke, Graham pushed herself up on the pile of pillows at the head of the bed, exhausted but content. Anna lay curled around her, her head resting against Graham's shoulder.

"Will you pour us some champagne now, my love?" Graham asked.

Anna kissed her, loathe to move away even for an instant. "Of course, darling."

Graham sipped the fine wine and sighed. "Are you sure that this is what you want? For a lifetime? I can be—difficult."

"Graham Yardley. I would never have thought you capable of such understatement." Anna laughed softly, tenderly caressing Graham's cheek. Serious again, she swept her lips across Graham's. "I want this and much, much more."

Graham raised an eyebrow, her face questioning. "And exactly what are your requirements? Perhaps I should consider them before we proceed any further."

Again she laughed, rejoicing in the return of the light in Graham's eyes. "First of all, I want to see you well again," Anna stated quietly.

Graham looked uncomfortable, turning her face away. "It's nothing that having you here won't cure."

"Tell me about it, Graham. I'm with you now. Please let me help," Anna urged, pulling Graham close against her.

"After you left, I couldn't stay at Yardley. Nothing, not even losing my sight, was as devastating as losing you." Graham's voice was low and halting. Just recounting the desolation of those days was agonizing.

"Oh, my darling," Anna cried, near tears. "I'm so sorry. Never, never did I mean to hurt you so." Had she not come now, had Graham not recovered. "Oh God," she gasped involuntarily, unable to bear the thought.

"Shh, my love. It's over now," Graham soothed, silencing Anna with a kiss. "All that matters is that you are here." She didn't tell Anna of how close she had been to death, and how death had seemed like a welcome friend, offering her surcease from a loneliness she could no longer endure. But though her soul had longed for delivery, her body had rallied, and although weak, she was indeed recovering.

"I will never leave you, Graham. You have my promise. Please, I want to go home, to Yardley. I want to live with you there, and I want to hear you play for me again. Please take me home."

"I will, my love," Graham murmured, her lips finding Anna's, finally daring to hope that love could be hers.

CHAPTER TWENTY

They look good," Anna called as she pulled the Jeep along side Daphne and her crew. She indicated the new shrubs the women were putting in beside the entrance at Yardley.

Daphne leaned down to the window, smiling at her boss. "They're great specimens. We should be done here soon, then I thought we'd start the plantings on the rear terrace tomorrow. The photographers will be out on Friday to shoot the front gardens."

Anna raised a shoulder nonchalantly. "Whatever you decide."

Daphne grinned. "The view is better from the terrace, too. If you're watching women."

Anna caught the mischievous glint in her eye, and replied smartly, "You had better not be talking about Graham. And besides, I thought you were happily married."

Daphne laughed. "Completely domesticated, and even if I weren't, I know better than to lust after Graham. She doesn't know there's another woman on earth besides you, and you'd have my hide just for the thought. I was talking about my new kid, Lori. She's got a bad case for Graham's assistant. She seems to find all kinds of excuses to wander by the music room when they're working."

Anna glanced at her watch. It was almost five in the afternoon. "Are Graham and Sheila still at it? They were up most of the night. Graham promised me she'd get some rest," she finished worriedly. The memory of the long agonizing months alone in Boston still lingered. Graham's recent illness left her terrified that something would take Graham from her.

Daphne saw the fear flicker across Anna's face, and remembered how frail Graham had seemed not long ago. She reflected on the change six months had brought. "Anna," she said softly, "Graham looks great. I've never seen her like she is now. She's strong and healthy. And the music that comes out of that room. I have to practically drag my crew from the terrace."

Anna forced herself to relax, knowing what Daphne said was true. "It's helped Graham to have Sheila here. She's transcribing Graham's new work and cataloging her unpublished pieces. It's just that the two of them can get lost when they're working. Sheila's almost as bad as Graham."

"She's writing her graduate thesis on Graham's compositions, right?"

"Yes. Actually, she's a student-in-residence with Graham for the rest of the year." Anna could scarcely believe it when Graham had asked her to contact the graduate student who had written so many times requesting an interview. Sheila had been with them for two months and had quickly become devoted to Graham. Not only was her musicological assistance invaluable, it soon became apparent that she had an innate appreciation of Graham's other needs as well. She dealt with Graham's blindness in an understated way that did not impinge on Graham's need for independence. Anna trusted her with her most valuable possession—her lover's well being.

"Well a year ought to give Lori enough time to win Sheila's heart," Daphne mused.

Anna laughed. "You have a one-track mind."

"Oh, and you don't?" Daphne rejoined.

Anna blushed, recalling the urge she had had on the drive home to feel Graham's hands on her body. Even now she couldn't believe the turn her life had taken. She hadn't imagined she could be this happy. She put the Jeep in gear and pulled away smiling.

She tapped lightly at the partially open door to the music room. She stood quietly listening when she got no response, knowing it was Graham playing without needing to look. Graham said that Sheila was a very gifted musician, but Anna never confused the two. When Graham played, the combination of grace and power was unmistakable. It was her signature, a complete reflection of her self. Anna knew the cadence and the rhythm of her music with the same certainty as she knew the sound of her voice, or her caress.

She entered and watched from across the room. Graham was moving over the keys, the notes flowing from her hands, her essence transformed into sound. It still took Anna's breath away and often kindled desire so intense that she shook. She cleared her throat as the refrain ended and called, "Hey, you two. Are you ready to take a break any time soon?"

Graham swiveled toward her, smiling a greeting. "You're home early, aren't you, love?"

She looked fresh and energized, a sure sign that her work was going well. She clearly had no idea of the time, and Anna was willing to bet they hadn't stopped for lunch. Anna cast a stern glance at Sheila, who shrugged her shoulders sheepishly as she sidled toward the door, clearly hoping for a swift escape.

"You're both impossible," Anna muttered. She crossed the room to Graham, draping her arms around her from behind, breathing a kiss into her hair. Graham reached up to cover Anna's hands where they lay lightly stroking her chest. She turned Anna's palm up, pressing her lips to the soft skin before resting her cheek in the curve of Anna's hand. She sighed contentedly.

"I'm glad you're home," she murmured.

"Are you all right?" Anna whispered, tightening her hold on the woman who meant more to her than her very life.

"Fine," Graham replied. "But I have news."

"What?"

Graham hesitated, her fingers caressing Anna's, the expression on her face contemplative. "I have agreed to give a performance for the symphony in July."

Anna gasped. "Oh darling, that's wonderful." It was more than she had ever imagined possible.

"You don't mind?" Graham asked in a subdued tone. "It won't be a problem?"

Anna slid onto the piano bench beside Graham, slipping an arm about her waist. "What makes you think I would mind?" she asked quietly.

"It will mean I'll be working more, and when I'm preparing for a performance, I tend to get absorbed."

Anna thought she understood what Graham wasn't saying. "And you think I'll come to resent that?"

"Perhaps."

"Graham," Anna began carefully, "I know what you're like when you work, and sometimes I do worry, but not about us—about you. You forget to eat, you forget to sleep, you lose weight you don't have to spare. I have never felt, not once, that I didn't matter to you—or that you had stopped loving me, even for a moment."

"I couldn't stop loving you, not and still draw a breath," Graham whispered, her fingers tightening their grip on Anna's. "You are my light, and my heart. You are the reason there is music in my life again."

"As long as that is true, we'll be fine," Anna assured her. "But you must promise me that you will take care of yourself. I need you so much, Graham. Without you—there's no point—"

Graham stilled her words with a kiss. "I promise, my love."

There was something else. Anna could sense it in the tension of Graham's body, in the quiet tone of her voice. Something worried her lover still.

"Now tell me the rest," she ordered gently, fitting herself closer against Graham's side.

"If I perform," Graham began hesitantly, then finished firmly, "if I perform, I know what will happen. I've been there before, Anna. There's no point pretending it won't create an uproar. Once I make an appearance, the demands for my time will intensify. There will be pressure for me to tour."

Anna took her time, thinking of the ramifications of Graham's words. She welcomed the changes in Graham over the last months. Graham was suffused with energy, her creative powers seemingly unleashed by the security of Anna's presence. She was vital, dynamic, almost intoxicating in her passionate embrace of life. Her ardor for Anna, her muse, was boundless. Anna hadn't imagined she could be this happy. Now she was faced with the reality of Graham's true place in the world.

Graham was a peerless artist, one whom the world would not let go lightly yet again. If she returned to the concert stage, she would be resuming the life she had led before Anna. What Anna said now would determine the course of both their lives, and she warred with feelings of both love and fear. She adored Graham, adored her genius, and she wanted her to celebrate her talent as it should be expressed. But she loved the woman, and feared for her—for the tender spirit that gave so much to the music. She could not lose her, for Graham was life itself to her.

Graham took her silence to mean Anna was opposed to the idea. "It's no matter," Graham said decisively. "I'll simply tell them no."

"You can't do that, Graham. And I wouldn't ask you to," Anna began quietly. "I love you, and I have always known who you are— what you are. You don't belong just to me—"

"I *do* belong just to you," Graham interrupted fiercely.

Anna laughed gently, resting her hand possessively on Graham's thigh. "I know *that*, my darling. I was talking about your music. I wouldn't keep you from it, and you can't keep it from the world." She took a deep, certain breath. "You'll perform again, and you'll have to tour, Graham."

Graham stood, pacing by the piano, formulating plans. Anna realized that except for her blindness, Graham was very nearly the woman she had been before her accident. When she stepped onto the stage, her return would be complete. She was about to reclaim the world she once ruled, and Anna could see that it was destined. Graham was transformed before her eyes into the impresario she had only glimpsed in faded newspaper clippings. It was breathtaking, and a little terrifying.

Graham ran a hand through her hair, thinking aloud. "Sheila would almost certainly want to come. That would be a great help. I can limit foreign travel, but it's still going to be unbearable being apart from you even for a short time."

Anna rose, stilling Graham's restless motion with a hand on her arm. She grasped her about the waist, holding her firmly. "You can't think I'd let you go without me? Not only would I go mad with worry, I have no intention of leaving you unattended with all those glamorous society women. You seem to have no idea of the effect you have on women, but I certainly do."

Graham looked at her in confusion. "You can't think I could ever want anyone but you? Don't you know you are my life?"

"I'm not taking any chances," Anna uttered as she kissed her swiftly, possessively.

"But your job?"

"I'll try to work something out with Lauren when the time comes. Maybe I can freelance for her—work part time. I don't know. I don't care. Where you need to be is where I'll be. You're what I need."

Graham pulled her near, admitting in a low voice, "I'm not worried about the music—that's never been the hard part. But the people—the promoters, the agents, the press—they want so much from me. It's hard to keep from being consumed. I'm not sure I can do it again—especially now, when I can't see."

It was so unlike Graham to voice any concern, particularly regarding her blindness, Anna was instantly protective. She tightened her hold, her voice unflinching. "You won't have to worry; you're not alone any more."

The tension finally eased from Graham's body as she gentled under Anna's caresses. She kissed Anna lingeringly, before murmuring quietly, "Thank you for my life, Anna."

Anna grasped the slender fingers that made magic the entire world demanded. She drew them to her breast, where they played only for her. "You can thank me upstairs," she whispered urgently. Graham lowered her lips to Anna's ear as she stroked her tauntingly, teasing her nipples through the thin cotton of her shirt.

"A command performance—my favorite thing."

"It had better be," Anna gasped. "And I can't wait any longer for you to begin."

Graham's laughter echoed through the halls as she led her love to their bed.

CHAPTER TWENTY-ONE

What time will the car be here, dear?" Helen asked anxiously for the third time since Anna had arrived home early from work.

"Five-thirty," Anna replied with a smile.

"My goodness, it's one o'clock. I'd better get ready."

"You have plenty of time. You'll end up waiting," Anna suggested as if it would make a difference.

"I've been waiting nearly fifteen years for this. A few hours is nothing. I still think we should take the Bentley. Graham always went to a performance in the Bentley."

"I know, Helen," Anna said patiently. "But Graham wanted it this way."

"Well, I guess it will be all right then," Helen relented. Then she continued with concern, "You did interview the chauffeur?"

Anna laughed. "I did, and it's a woman. She understands exactly what we need. It will be perfect."

"And you double checked that the invitations went out for the reception? I could have done that, you know. I always did that before."

"I know," Anna replied gently, "and I would have been lost without your help this time. I know they arrived, because Lauren got hers. It was more important that you look after Graham." Anna was nearly as anxious as Helen, and she desperately needed to see Graham. "Now, where is she?"

"She's upstairs in the master suite. Max brought your gown and her suit. I had them sent up."

"Good. How does she seem?"

"Calm. She slept late. She didn't even practice. She rarely did the day of a performance. The barber has come and gone. Oh, I do hope it goes well. This is so important to her."

"Helen," Anna reminded her with conviction, "this is what Graham was born for. Don't worry, she'll be magnificent."

"You believe that, don't you?"

"Absolutely. I know it."

"I give thanks every day that you came to us," Helen whispered, tears in her eyes.

Anna hugged her. "No more than I."

She entered their bedroom to find her lover reclining in one of the chairs before the open window. She was in a black silk thigh length dressing jacket, looking impossibly relaxed. And impossibly beautiful. In repose, her features always reminded Anna of a classical sculpture— cool, remote, elegantly refined. It was the same handsome face that looked back at her from the posters all over the city announcing Graham's concert that night. Anna admired her from a distance before Graham's expression softened with recognition at the sound of her step on the parquet floor.

"Hello, my love," Graham called softly.

"Hello, darling. What were you just thinking of?"

Graham looked surprised. "The music."

Anna settled onto the arm of Graham's chair, resting her fingers in the thick hair at the base of Graham's neck. She leaned to give her a swift kiss. "I should have guessed."

"Why?" Graham asked, pulling Anna down into her lap.

"Because you looked like you were lost somewhere, somewhere no one can follow."

"Does that bother you?" Graham murmured as her lips sought the sensitive spot beneath Anna's ear.

"It might," Anna breathed as she turned her lips to Graham's.

The kiss deepened, and soon they were both gasping. Anna's head felt light and her body burned. "If I couldn't call you back to me," she said, her voice husky with desire.

Graham got to her feet, pulling Anna up into her arms. "You can always call me back," she whispered against the warm skin of Anna's neck. "Because I am yours." With one hand she held Anna close, with the other she parted the front of Anna's blouse, slipping her hand inside to cup her breast.

Anna groaned, feeling the length of Graham's naked thigh pressing against her. "Graham, stop—we can't—you need to get ready." She gasped as Graham's hand dropped lower, finding her rising heat. "Oh no—that's not fair. You make me want you so much."

Graham laughed, pulling Anna toward the bed. "Don't you know I've been waiting all morning for this? You are the only thing I need right now."

"Is that some sort of pre-performance ritual?" Anna asked as she toweled off from the shower. Graham's lovemaking was always a reflection of her emotional state, and this time she had been explosively intense, consuming in her hunger.

Graham grinned. "Now there's an idea. It certainly could be arranged."

"It did wonders for my nerves," Anna said with a smile. "How are yours?"

Graham held out a perfectly steady hand as her grin deepened. "Just fine. Where are the studs for my shirt?"

"On your dresser—just to the right of your brushes." Anna watched the graceful fingers expertly fit the small mother-of-pearl studs through the holes in the starched formal shirt—the same fingers that just an hour ago had claimed her, relentlessly, until they had drawn the last trembling shudders from her body.

"You're watching me," Graham remarked, reaching for the white silk tie. She turned the length of it in her fingers, orienting it so she could tie it.

Anna laughed softly, drawing the delicate fabric into her hands, reaching up to fit it around her lover's neck.

"Was I doing that wrong?" Graham asked, her face puzzled.

"You never do anything wrong," Anna admonished gently. "I'm doing it because it pleases me to do it." She finished the knot and brushed a kiss across Graham's lips. "I love you, and I'm so proud of you."

Graham returned the kiss, her expression serious. "I love you with all my heart. Now, tell me about your dress. I want to have a picture of you in my mind tonight."

Anna stepped away, lifting the flowing fabric from the hanger, settling it over her body. "Why don't you come see for yourself," she teased.

A faint smile flickered at the corner of Graham's fine mouth. No one in her life could command her the way Anna did. "All right."

She crossed to Anna, who stood still as Graham gently traced the material that fell from her shoulders, following the lines along her bodice and down to her waist. Her exploring touch rekindled the fire in Anna's belly, and she battled the urge to draw those gently stroking fingers to her again. They absolutely did not have time for this now.

"And the color?" Graham murmured huskily, her hands resting on Anna's hips.

"Midnight—on a clear night in October," Anna managed, sliding her arms around Graham's neck.

Graham nodded, holding her close. "Beautiful."

Anna touched a finger to her own lips, then to Graham's. "Thank you."

They rode in silence to the symphony hall. Anna's hand rested gently in Graham's. Graham's hand was warm and steady. As they slowed to glide up to the curb, Anna glanced out the window.

"Tell me," Graham said calmly.

"There are a lot of people. Quite a number of photographers. The sidewalk is roped off, though."

"How far?" came the quiet question.

"The same distance as from our front door to your music room. Four steps up—then five paces to the door. Sheila is waiting inside to walk you back stage to your dressing room."

Graham didn't ask how Anna knew the precise distance she would have to travel in front of a curious crowd, a walk she had taken so many times before, but never in darkness. She didn't ask, because in her heart she knew.

Anna had been there the day before, walking the route Graham would take just to be certain. She couldn't even begin to imagine how difficult this first public appearance since the accident must be for Graham. She wanted to make it as easy for her as she could. She squeezed Graham's hand reassuringly. "I love you."

"Thank you," Graham said softly, "for more than I can say."

"We're here," Anna said as the limo halted. "You can do this easily by yourself, Graham."

"Yes," Graham said as she pushed the limo door open, stepping out to a barrage of camera flashes and a cacophony of voices calling to her. "Ms. Yardley! Maestra! Over here!"

Oblivious to the demands of the crowd, she reached down and handed Anna from the car, tucking Anna's hand firmly into the curve of her arm. "But I don't have to do it alone any longer, do I?" she whispered to Anna as they turned and began the walk Graham was born to make.

The concert hall was filled to capacity. The news of Graham's return to the concert stage had created a stir in the music world, and her performance was eagerly awaited. Anna sat with Helen, trying to quell her nerves. They were in the VIP box to the left of the stage, seats that were situated so one could watch the pianist's hands on the keyboard. Shortly after they were seated a young usher approached, a bouquet of long-stemmed white roses in his arms. He stopped before Anna, saying, "For you, madam."

Anna cradled the flowers, opening the card with trembling hands. In Graham's bold hand the message read, "You are my strength and my inspiration. *You are my heart. All the music is for you. Yours eternally,* Graham."

"Oh, Graham," she murmured, tears suddenly wetting her cheeks.

"Are you all right, dear?" Helen asked in concern.

Anna took her hand, squeezing it gently while she tried to contain her tears. "When I think that I could have lost her—that we all might have lost her. Oh, Helen."

Helen patted her hand reassuringly. "You needn't worry, Anna. She's stronger for having you than ever she was before the accident."

The house lights dimmed and suddenly Graham was on stage— tall, elegant, perfectly composed. She bowed once in acknowledgement to the orchestra and the audience, then settled herself before the piano as if she had never been away.

Anna watched the slender form bend to the strains of the music filling the hall, a refrain that carried to those who listened all the beauty and tender passion of Graham's heart. At last she witnessed what she had only imagined from faded images in a dusty scrapbook. Alone in the muted spotlight, center stage, the impresario gifted them with her genius. The audience was on its feet just as the last notes faded away, some throwing single roses onto the stage, welcoming Graham home. Graham stood to acknowledge the applause, turning toward the seats where she knew Anna sat. She bowed first to her, one hand to her heart, offering her thanks. Through her tears, Anna looked into the dark eyes that she knew could see into her very soul.

When finally the ovation began to abate, Graham left the stage, and found herself immediately surrounded by people requesting a statement or an interview. A hand unobtrusively took her elbow, steadying her in the jostling crowd.

"Let's get back to your dressing room," Sheila suggested. She had been waiting offstage at Anna's request. They both knew what would happen the moment Graham appeared in the wings. There would be no way for her to orient herself there, especially when she would be exhausted from the rigors of her performance.

"Where is Anna?" Graham asked immediately, grateful for Sheila's presence in the demanding press of people.

"She's coming," Sheila replied grimly as she shouldered a path through a throng of reporters and fans. The excited crowd was at a fever pitch, everyone wanting to get to Graham, pushing forward despite the security people's best efforts. It was worse than Sheila expected, and she was beginning to fear for Graham's safety.

Suddenly the hallway in front of them began to clear as Anna's vehement voice rang out, "Everyone will have a chance to speak with her at the reception—and not *until* then. Now if you'll just give us a moment alone, please."

And then she was there, with Graham, the only place she ever wanted to be.

"Thank you, Sheila," Anna said quietly as she stepped up to Graham, not caring that dozens of people surrounded them. She reached for Graham's hand and brought it gently to her lips. "Hello, darling."

Graham lifted her free hand to Anna's cheek. It was still moist with tears. "Hello, my love." She drew Anna gently near and rested her forehead against Anna's hair. She closed her eyes with a sigh.

"Were you pleased?" Graham asked at last.

"Much more than pleased," Anna answered. "The only thing in this world I love more than your music is you." She stepped back with effort, for all she wanted to do was hold onto her.

Graham's jacket and shirt were soaked with sweat, and for the first time all day, her hands trembled. Anna slipped an arm about her waist.

"Let's get you out of here," Anna said, looking over her shoulder at the amazingly quiet group in the corridor. "Sheila, tell them ten minutes please."

When the dressing room door finally closed behind them, Anna drew off Graham's coat and loosened her tie.

"You needn't do that, Anna," Graham protested when Anna began pulling the studs from her shirt.

"Graham, hush," Anna said in exasperation. "I'll give you up to the demands of your music when I must, but not for one minute longer. You need a dry shirt and jacket if you're going to the reception." She brushed the damp hair back from Graham's face with concern. "Are you up to it? Because I'll just tell them all to be damned if you're too tired."

Graham grasped her hands. "I'm fine. And I would appreciate a dry shirt very much."

"Thank you for the flowers," Anna said softly as she fitted the diamond cufflinks into Graham's sleeves. "You make me feel so loved."

"I couldn't do this—any of this, without you," Graham murmured, exhausted from her performance. "I'll never be able to tell you how much I love you—"

"You don't have to tell me," Anna whispered, "I can see it in your face, and in the way you touch me, and in the music that you write." She paused her ministrations to slide her fingers into Graham's hair, pulling her head down for a kiss. After a moment she said gently, "Now stand still so I can fix this tie."

As Anna straightened her tie, Graham asked quietly, "Will you be all right in there? There are likely to be questions—about us. There was always speculation about Christine."

"If they don't know after my little scene in the hall, they never will," Anna laughed tightly. She hated to be reminded that once Christine had shared moments like these with Graham. She still grew angry whenever she remembered the kiss she had witnessed in the library. "And I couldn't give a damn about their questions. There—now you are your handsome self. Let's go finish your duties so I can take you home."

Lauren maneuvered through the crush of people toward Anna. She had been trying unsuccessfully to catch Anna's attention since she entered with Graham. She soon realized that would be impossible. Even though Anna was separated from Graham by a roomful of people, she managed to carry on polite conversation while never taking her eyes off her tall lover. Lauren knew how frightened Anna had been by Graham's recent illness, and she doubted that anything would distract her from her ever-vigilant watch over her now.

The instant Graham arrived, she was surrounded and swept away by luminaries from the music community and the ever-present press. In a throng like this she was quite helpless to fend off anyone who wanted her attention. Graham looked calm and remotely detached, but Lauren could imagine the effort it required for her to satisfy the escalating demands of those gathered about her. And she was quite sure that Anna had no intention of allowing Graham to be inundated like this for long.

"Thanks for the invitation to the reception," Lauren managed when at last she reached Anna's side. She slipped her arm around the pretty redhead at her side. "Anna, this is Lisa McCleary. Lisa is a music instructor at UMass, as well as—well, my—"

"Girlfriend," Lisa finished for her with a kilowatt smile.

Anna smiled with true pleasure, offering her hand. "It sounds trite to say I've heard a lot about you, but I'm glad to have finally met you."

"And I you," Lisa responded. "I guess I don't need to tell you how exciting this is, to have Graham Yardley performing again. She's wonderful."

"Isn't she," Anna responded, her eyes returning to where Graham stood. At that moment she was in deep conversation with the governor, who appeared to be as enchanted with her as everyone else in the room. "Even I can say that without prejudice," she laughed softly. "I'm so glad you both could come. Lauren has had to excuse my distractibility a good deal lately. I think I've been more anxious than Graham."

"It sounds like you didn't need to be. From what I'm hearing around the room, she's even better than before. I don't know how that's possible, but I've never heard anyone like her."

"Yes," Anna said simply. "And I think she's probably worked enough for one night. Will you excuse me while I attempt a rescue?"

Before she could move away, a reporter blocked her path. "Ms. Reid, is it true that you are Graham Yardley's lover?" he asked bluntly.

Anna appraised him coolly, leaning forward slightly to read the name on the press card pinned to his lapel. "Mr. Phillips," she replied calmly, "Graham Yardley is inarguably one of the greatest artists of this century. I would think that fact alone would offer much more of interest to your readers than speculation about her personal life."

"Am I to take it then that you deny any intimate relationship with her?" he persisted, a smug grin on his face.

"There is nothing about my relationship with Graham I would deny," Anna answered firmly, "least of all my love."

"And is it also true that Christine Hunt-Blair was once her lover as well?"

Anna fixed him with a steely stare. "You would have to ask Mrs. Hunt-Blair about their past relationship." She pointedly turned her back, determined not to reveal her wrath at the mention of Christine. Would she never be done hearing of that woman? As Anna wended her way slowly across the crowded room, Graham was approached by yet another admirer. From where she was, Anna could only watch, anger combining with an unexpected surge of possessiveness.

"Hello, darling," a sultry voice beside Graham murmured as a hand trailed down her arm in a flagrant caress.

Graham turned to the woman beside her, lifting the hand from her sleeve with a slight bow. "Hello, Christine," Graham said neutrally.

"You were magnificent, as usual." Christine purred, stepping close enough for Graham to catch the scent of her perfume. Her breasts lightly grazed Graham's chest.

"Thank you," Graham replied, raising her head, casting a glance about the room. Her eyes fell so unerringly on her lover in the midst of the crowd, anyone looking at her would have sworn that she could see. Graham relaxed perceptibly when she sensed an answering gaze upon her face.

"Why so formal, darling," Christine admonished, taking advantage of the crush of people to move closer still. She toyed with a stud on the front of Graham's shirt. "As I recall, you used to rather like my presence after a performance. As a matter of fact, you were quite demanding about your requirements. I remember you could barely wait to get me alone. Not that I minded of course. You were always at your best after a concert." As she spoke, she curled her fingers ever so slightly under the waistband of Graham's trousers.

"That was a long time ago," Anna said succinctly as she stepped to Graham's side, taking Graham's hand in hers, forcing Christine back a step. Graham laced her fingers gently through Anna's.

"Things are very different for Graham now," Anna continued, furious at Christine's suggestive remarks, but struggling for calm. This was no place for a scene, as dearly as she would like to make it clear that Christine had no rights to Graham any longer.

"But some things never change, do they Graham?" Christine questioned softly, her eyes on Graham's face, ignoring Anna entirely. Necessity had made her bold. This was her last chance to reclaim Graham—here, now, on the stage she had always shared with her.

"Don't tell me you've forgotten what it was like, darling. Adored by everyone—the celebrity, the excitement, the lovemaking. Don't expect me to believe you've forgotten that. I haven't forgotten, I could never forget." Her voice grew urgent, her expression desperate. "We could have it all again, Graham—just as it was, the two of us. You could have everything you ever wanted."

Graham tightened her hold on Anna, drawing her close against her side. "I already have everything I want—more than I ever dreamed possible. More than I deserve. What we had is over Christine. I have everything I need right here. Now, if you'll excuse us, I'd like Anna to take me home."

"I had the limo brought around back," Anna said as Christine stared after them in shock. "Just turn around and we can sneak out."

When they were settled at last in the expansive rear of the stretch limo, separated by a smoked-glass partition from the front seat where Helen sat happily directing the chauffeur, Graham spoke quietly. "I'm terribly sorry about Christine. I had no idea she would be there."

"I doubt there's any event where Christine Hunt-Blair is not invited," Anna said acerbically, reminding herself of her resolution to remain calm. She failed. "God, I *hate* the way she touches you. She acts like she owns you."

"Well, she doesn't. And she hasn't for a long time," Graham responded gently.

"Well, I wish someone would tell *her* that," Anna railed.

Graham raised an eyebrow. "I thought *I* just did," she said dryly.

Anna stared at her imperious lover, struggling to hold onto her anger. Helplessly, she laughed, moving closer to drape an arm around Graham's waist, pressing her face to Graham's neck. "Yes, you did."

In a calmer light she knew she would only pity Christine and her desperate attempt to renew her affair with Graham, but at the moment she was still stinging from the sight of Christine openly caressing *her* lover. She was a good deal less than rational where Graham was concerned, and not above making her claim very clear. She slipped a hand along the inside of Graham's thigh, smiling as Graham gasped at the light caress. "Was she serious about the effect a performance has on you?" she asked innocently, very aware of the tension in Graham's body.

"Yes," Graham said tightly as Anna's hand strayed higher. It would be useless to deny it; Anna could read her responses too well. She pressed back against the seat, torn between wanting Anna's touch to continue and trying to save some semblance of control.

"Now *that's* something you might have mentioned," Anna remarked as her fingers pressed a particularly sensitive spot, rubbing the faint prominence through the fabric. Her pulse hammered as she felt Graham shudder.

"Anna," Graham warned unconvincingly, struggling to maintain her composure. They were in a limousine, for God's sake.

"Definitely an unexpected benefit," Anna mused as if Graham hadn't spoken. She tormented her by touching her with no particular rhythm, stopping when she felt Graham's breath quicken, teasing her unmercifully. She wanted to be sure she had Graham's full attention.

"Why didn't you tell me?" she inquired as if asking the time, returning unerringly to the spot that caused Graham to quiver.

Graham groaned softly. "It wasn't foremost in my mind," she managed to gasp, completely under Anna's spell. She reached for Anna's hand, holding it to her, urging her to continue. "Ahh—God—"

"Is it now?" Anna questioned, increasing the pressure of her hand slightly. Graham moaned, a low strangled plea. Anna knew just how close Graham was to coming—she knew, and she pushed a little harder, grasping her between her fingers.

Graham shivered involuntarily, trembling in Anna's embrace. "Yes," she whispered, "please don't stop."

"Oh, I don't intend to stop," Anna breathed into her ear, easing her fingers away slightly, "not ever. But since I'm conducting this particular piece, you'll have to wait until we get home for the finale."

"Ah, Jesus," Graham rasped, her voice catching. "Is that a promise? Because you're killing me."

Anna held Graham fiercely, her lips urgent against her skin. "As I am yours, so are you mine. That's a pledge, and a promise, *my darling*."

The End

About the Author

Radclyffe is a member of the Golden Crown Literary Society, Pink Ink, the Romance Writers of America, and a two-time recipient of the Alice B. award for lesbian fiction. She has written numerous best-selling lesbian romances (*Safe Harbor* and its sequel *Beyond the Breakwater, Innocent Hearts, Love's Melody Lost, Love's Tender Warriors, Tomorrow's Promise, Passion's Bright Fury, Love's Masquerade, shadowland,* and *Fated Love*), two romance/intrigue series: the Honor series *(Above All, Honor, Honor Bound, Love & Honor,* and *Honor Guards)* and the Justice series (*Shield of Justice,* the prequel *A Matter of Trust, In Pursuit of Justice,* and *Justice in the Shadows)*, as well as an erotica collection: *Change of Pace – Erotic Interludes.*

She lives with her partner, Lee, in Philadelphia, PA where she both writes and practices surgery full-time. She is also the president of Bold Strokes Books, a lesbian publishing company.

Her upcoming works include: *Justice Served* (June 2005); *Stolen Moments: Erotic Interludes 2,* ed. with Stacia Seaman (September 2005), and *Honor Reclaimed* (December 2005)

Look for information about these works at www.radfic.com and www.boldstrokesbooks.com.

Other Books Available From Bold Strokes Books

Course of Action by Gun Brooke. Actress Carolyn Black desperately wants the starring role in an upcoming film produced by Annelie Peterson, a wealthy publisher with a mysterious past. How far is Carolyn prepared to go for the dream part of a lifetime? And just how far will Annelie bend her principles in the name of desire? (1-933110-22-8)

Rangers at Roadsend by Jane Fletcher. After nine years in the Rangers, dealing with thugs and wild predators, Sergeant Chip Coppelli has learned to spot trouble coming, and that is exactly what she sees in her new recruit, Katryn Nagata. But even so, Chip was not expecting murder. The Celaeno series. (1-933110-28-7)

Justice Served by Radclyffe. The hunt for an informant in the ranks draws Lieutenant Rebecca Frye, her lover Dr. Catherine Rawlings, and Officer Dellon Mitchell into a deadly game of hide-and-seek with an underworld kingpin who traffics in human souls. (1-933110-15-5)

Distant Shores, Silent Thunder by Radclyffe. Ex-lovers, would-be lovers, and old rivals find their paths unwillingly entwined when Doctors KT O'Bannon and Tory King—and the women who love them—are forced to examine the boundaries of love, friendship, and the ties that transcend time. (1-933110-08-2)

Hunter's Pursuit by Kim Baldwin. A raging blizzard, a remote mountain hideaway, and more than one killer-for-hire set a scene for disaster—or desire—when reluctant assassin Katarzyna Demetrious rescues a stranger and unwittingly exposes her heart. (1-933110-09-0)

The Walls of Westernfort by Jane Fletcher. All Temple Guard Natasha Ionadis wants is to serve the Goddess, and she volunteers eagerly for a dangerous mission to infiltrate a band of rebels. But once away from the temple, the issues are no longer so simple, especially in light of her attraction to one of the rebels. Is it too late to work out what she really wants from life? (1-933110-24-4)

Change Of Pace: *Erotic Interludes* by Radclyffe. Twenty-five hot-wired encounters guaranteed to spark more than just your imagination. Erotica as you've always dreamed of it. (1-933110-07-4)

Fated Love by Radclyffe. Amidst the chaos and drama of a busy emergency room, two women must contend not only with the fragile nature of life, but also with the mysteries of the heart and the irresistible forces of fate. (1-933110-05-8)

Justice in the Shadows by Radclyffe. In a shadow world of secrets, lies, and hidden agendas, Detective Sergeant Rebecca Frye and her lover, Dr. Catherine Rawlings, join forces once again in the elusive search for justice. (1-933110-03-1)

shadowland by Radclyffe. In a world on the far edge of desire, two women are drawn together by power, passion, and dark pleasures. An erotic romance. (1-933110-11-2)

Love's Masquerade by Radclyffe. Plunged into the often indistinguishable realms of fiction, fantasy, and hidden desires, Auden Frost discovers a shifting landscape that will force her to question everything she has believed to be true about herself and the nature of love. (1-933110-14-7)

Beyond the Breakwater by Radclyffe. One Provincetown summer three women learn the true meaning of love, friendship, and family. Second in the Provincetown Tales. (1-933110-06-6)

Tomorrow's Promise by Radclyffe. One timeless summer, two very different women discover the power of passion to heal and the promise of hope that only love can bestow. (1-933110-12-0)

Love's Tender Warriors by Radclyffe. Two women who have accepted loneliness as a way of life learn that love is worth fighting for and a battle they cannot afford to lose. (1-933110-02-3)

Love's Melody Lost by Radclyffe. A secretive artist with a haunted past and a young woman escaping a life that proved to be a lie find their destinies entwined. (1-933110-00-7)

Safe Harbor by Radclyffe. A mysterious newcomer, a reclusive doctor, and a troubled gay teenager learn about love, friendship, and trust during one tumultuous summer in Provincetown. First in the Provincetown Tales. (1-933110-13-9)

Above All, Honor by Radclyffe. The first in the Honor series introduces single-minded Secret Service Agent Cameron Roberts and the woman she is sworn to protect—Blair Powell, the daughter of the president of the United States. First in the Honor series. (1-933110-04-X)

Love & Honor by Radclyffe. The president's daughter and her security chief are faced with difficult choices as they battle a tangled web of Washington intrigue for...love and honor. Third in the Honor series. (1-933110-10-4)

Honor Guards by Radclyffe. In a journey that begins on the streets of Paris's Left Bank and culminates in a wild flight for their lives, the president's daughter and those who are sworn to protect her wage a desperate struggle for survival. Fourth in the Honor series. (1-933110-01-5)